Once a Grunt

Mike Ledingham

BMS Books
5 High Street
Rotorua, 3010
New Zealand

First Published in April 2013
Mike Ledingham
ISBN: 978-0-473-24022-6

Published in August 2013 by BMS Books
An imprint of Business Media Services Limited
5 High Street, Rotorua 3010
P.O. Box 6215, Whakarewarewa
Rotorua 3010, New Zealand
Tel: 64-7-349 4107
Email: ms@bms.co.nz
Web site: www.bms.co.nz
All rights reserved.

ISBN: 978-0-473-25315-8

Also published in Kindle
ISBN: 978-0-473-25316-5

ABOUT THE AUTHOR

Mike Ledingham has been a farmhand, soldier, real estate salesman, small business operator, armed security guard and caregiver. *Once a Grunt* is an offbeat collection of 10 short stories loosely based on his experiences in the Infantry and the SAS and beyond. They reflect his keen enjoyment of the funny side of life, his total lack of respect for bullies and self-important wallies, and his deep empathy with the underdog.

.

CONTENTS

Introduction   i

Glossary (military terms and slang)   iii

ARMY LIFE   1

Snaky Bit   3

Soldier Under Sentence   7

What the Bloody Hell Have I Got Myself Into?   31

Who Called the Cook a Bastard?   69

Two-and-a-Half Fingers Left   71

CIVVY STREET   77

The Balaclava   79

Never a Team that Couldn't be Beat   85

Give the Dog a Bone   99

To be Sure, To be Sure   113

Just Desserts   121

INTRODUCTION

I've never been a perfectly correct human being, politically or grammatically, and so it is with these stories. Any mistakes are all mine. I'm good at that, making mistakes. Been doing it all my life.

Some of these yarns may have been inspired by actual events, but they have been taken further in flights of fancy. So they are not true. I hope military people will forgive any faux pas – I have written from my memories of my own experiences, and you know what they say about your memory as you get older.

I hope these stories make the reader laugh, or even just crack a smile. God knows, there isn't enough of that in the world these days.

All I know is that when I get together with my army mates, we like to drink a bit and reminisce and laugh a lot. Enjoy!

Special thanks to family and friends for their support and help with this project, particularly my guinea pig, proof reader, suggestion maker and brother, Peter Ledingham.

Mike Ledingham

Glossary
(Military terms and slang)

Baggies.............Private soldiers (or lowest rank in other services)

Basics (of people) New recruits

Battalion............Large infantry unit made up of hundreds of soldiers

Cadre staff.........Training NCOs

Click...............1,000 metres

Concourse.........Obstacle course

Double.............Run (like hell, at times)

Gonk...............Sleep

Grunt...............Infantryman

Gunners............Artillerymen

Hexamine.........Solid fuel blocks for heating the army's epicurean field rations

Hinu...............Fat

Losing your hook..Being demoted

Mess fatigues......Banging the pots (doing the dishes) at the mess

MOD...............Ministry of Defence

NAAFI..............Navy, Army and Air Force Institutes (organisation that runs messes and other military recreational facilities)

National Service...Compulsory military training (abolished in NZ in 1974)

O Group............Meeting of commanders

ORs' mess..........Dining facilities for junior NCOs and private soldiers ("other ranks")

Pap................Papakura military camp

Para...............Parachute or parachutist

Platoon..........Infantry unit usually made up of three sections of eight to 10 men

PTSU.............Parachute Training Support Unit

RF................Regular Force (as distinct from Territorial Force)

RFL..............Required fitness level

RIs..............Running instructions – military version of vehicle log book

RL................Bedford truck

RTU..............Returned to unit

RTNZ............Return to NZ

RV...............Rendezvous

Section..........Group of eight to 10 infantrymen, part of a platoon

Sig..............Signaller

Sign.............Tracks on ground

Squadron........The SAS (definition in the context of these stories)

Staff (as a title)..Staff Sergeant – rank between Sergeant and Warrant Officer Class II (Sergeant Major)

Stick.............Group of parachutists

TCs..............Tough cunts

TF...............Territorial Force

The J............The jungle

Waiouru.........Central North Island military camp, also known as the arsehole of NZ

WO1............Warrant Officer Class I

WRAC......... Female soldier

ARMY LIFE

SNAKY BIT

For my old army and drinking mate Poi.
"Yea, though he leadeth me down to the Empire to drink and to
gamble, I shall fear no evil. For he is still one mean fish." – ML

The patrol had been out for five days and hadn't found a thing. They'd grown bored and started to switch off, which could be dangerous if there was a sudden encounter with the enemy. The operation started after a local reported seeing three or four armed men crossing a stream. The whole area had been divided up into Areas of Operation, with each platoon given one to search. Because their AO was quite large, 3 Platoon's commander had decided to break it up into three section-size lots, with the strict proviso that as soon as any sign was found, the patrol would wait to be reinforced by at least one other section before following up. None of the sections had so far reported any sign and it looked like 3 Platoon was going to be shit out of luck on this occasion. They'd all be thoroughly pissed off if one of the other platoons got the lucky break and ended up making contact. They'd never hear the bloody end of it.

The patrol crossed a smallish, fairly clean, fast-running stream and about 25 metres into the jungle on the other side, the corporal decided to have a 30-minute brew stop and take the opportunity to refill their water bottles. The clear water was far less likely to give them the screaming shits.

He whistled quietly to get the rest of the patrol's attention, made the necessary hand signals and with the ease of constant practice, the section moved quietly and efficiently into all-round defence. As there had been no sign behind them, the corporal decided the sentry should watch the uncovered ground directly in front of the machine gun. Tail-end Charlie would have his usual and important job of watching their rear, but from within the section perimeter.

After a five minute stand-to – lie still, observe your arc and listen to see if anyone is about or following – they moved into the usual routine: Sentry out then brew up. It was old hat and boring but it was good to have a rest, a hot brew and of course the smokers could have a quick gasp. They were beginning to run out of essentials now – sugar and chocolate, the energy providers, as well as tobacco. Most of the guys smoked only when they were in "the J" to help them to allay hunger pangs, settle their nerves, or both (although most would die before admitting to nerves).

You could only carry so much food while on patrol and it was even worse this time. The hierarchy had decided that because they were in such small groups, it wouldn't pay to draw attention to themselves by bringing in fresh supplies by chopper. So they had to carry what they could and make it last, which guaranteed some pretty scant meals towards the end of the patrol.

The guys always brewed up in pairs and when the sentry was relieved after 15 minutes, his offsider would always have a hot brew ready for him. After some 10 minutes of peace, quiet and rest, the cover scout, Brand, signalled the corporal that he was going to take a leak off to the right, where a small bank was partially visible through the thick undergrowth. The corp gave him the thumbs up and Brand ambled off, SLR pointed downwards, magazine resting on ammo pouch, right hand resting lightly on pistol grip – the eternal stance of the rifleman.

The patrol were all gratefully sucking on their brews and puffing on their smokes when a blood-curdling scream erupted. There was a mad scramble as each soldier threw himself on to the ground. With weapons in shoulders, hearts pounding furiously, eyes anxiously scanning their arcs, they wondered what the fuck was going on. The sentry came sprinting in within seconds and threw himself into his allotted space. After an ever so long 25 seconds of quietness, the corporal yelled: "BRAND! BRAND! YOU OKAY?"

"NO!" came the shaky reply. "A fuckin' snake! Bastard whacked me right on the knob!" With that, Brand staggered into view, fly undone, penis hanging out. He stopped in front of the corp pointing to the dangling member which had a trickle of blood plus a slight smear of a clear-looking mucus.

"Lie down! Lie down!" ordered the corporal immediately, forcing Brand to the ground. Then he turned and snapped to the 2IC: "Sentries out both ends. Everyone observe their arcs. Tell the medic to come up." He turned back to the stricken soldier while the 2IC scurried away to carry out his orders.

The section commander removed Brand's rifle from his grip, checked the safety and placed it out of the way. He turned back to the patient, whose panic-filled eyes were fixed on his wound.

"Did you see the snake? What colour was it?" the corporal asked. "Only after it bit me," said Brand. "It was a long, thin, black bastard with orange and yellow on it." The corporal's heart sank. If a snake had bright stripes, it was usually a warning to stay away because it was venomous.

The section medic bustled up and the corporal told him: "Wash it down thoroughly with water and keep him quiet and calm. If the snake was venomous, him panicking will only pump it through the body all that much quicker. I'll get on the blower. We'll see if we can get a chopper in."

He turned to the unfortunate patient. "Take it easy Brand," he said. "The worst thing you can do now is panic. We'll get you out of here as soon as we can."

There was a bit on sniggering from the closest pair of soldiers now that the tension had eased – well, for most of them, anyway. "Shut up, you guys!" snapped the corporal. "It could just as easily been you, you know. Observe your bloody arcs." But he did have a bit of a lopsided grin on his face himself. There was a funny side to the situation.

He walked over to the sig and instructed him to call platoon HQ. The platoon commander agreed that Brand needed to be got out ASAP and told the corporal get straight through to base if he could. The commander could do nothing immediately to assist.

The corporal soon found himself talking directly to the medical officer.

"He needs to be medivaced ASAP," the doc was saying. "It's just a pity you couldn't kill the snake, then we'd know for sure, but I agree that it's probably venomous. Anyway, you'll soon know by his body's reaction to it."

The doctor continued: "The problem is that a bad batch of fuel has grounded several choppers, and a big contact up north has taken the rest out of our area for now. There probably won't be one available at least till tomorrow morning. Listen carefully, corporal.

This might sound like a hoary old chestnut, but it does have some sense to it and it's what I want you to do. You ready?"

"Yes, doc, fire away," said the corporal.

"Do you have plenty of water?" the doc asked. "We're right by a stream," the corporal replied.

"Good, get two of your biggest mess tins, fill 'em up with water and put 'em on to boil. You got that?"

"Doc."

"When they're boiling, put a scalpel from the med kit into one and two of the cleanest scraps of cloth you've got into the other, and boil 'em both for at least five minutes. Got that?"

"Doc."

"Wash the wound and the surrounding area thoroughly with one of the scraps of cloth, then take the scalpel and make a small incision into the bite marks until they're bleeding copiously. Got that?"

"Doc."

"Okay, now this is the crunch bit. Place your lips over the wound and suck as hard as you can and taking great care not to swallow. Spit everything out. Do this two or three times then make sure you thoroughly rinse your mouth out with water. Got that?"

"Doc." The corporal was shuddering by now.

"Okay, then take the second cloth out of the mess tin and wash the whole affected area. It will hurt, but tell Brand it's for his own good. Pour disinfectant over the area, bind it up with a bandage and keep him as quiet as possible. Tell him we'll definitely get him out tomorrow. Now have you got all that, corporal?"

"Doc," said the corporal. He did not much like the sound of what he had to do.

"Right, away you go and get on to it. Tell your medic to keep him quiet, keep reassuring him and to monitor his vital signs. Get straight back on to us if you're worried."

"Okay, doc," replied the by now very reluctant corporal.

He gave the handset back to the sig and trudged over to the patient, who looked bluish, pale and anxious. "What'd he say, corp?"

The corporal shook his head sadly. "He said you're probably gonna fuckin' die."

SOLDIER UNDER SENTENCE

"Prisoner and escort! About . . . turn! Double march! Left, right, left, right, left, right, get your knees up higher! Higher! That's better! Right . . . wheel! Mark time! Left, right, left, right, get 'em up! Get 'em up! Prisoner and escort! Halt!"

The prisoner and his two escorts halted and stood stock-still, heads up, eyes gazing fixedly at a spot high on Bullshit Castle wall, scarcely even daring to breathe.

"Escort! Dis...missed!" snapped the WO1. The two escorts turned sharply right, marched a couple of paces then disappeared quickly and thankfully. Not too many privates liked being round Bullshit Castle. There were simply too many people with rank, mostly clerical clowns, who wouldn't hesitate to give a sharp-end soldier a hard time for some real or imagined misdemeanour.

The battalion regimental sergeant major closed with the prisoner until their faces were nearly touching. "Do you understand your punishment, private? You've been awarded 60 days' confinement, which means you'll be transported to Ardmore Military Prison to serve your sentence."

"Yes, sah!" said the prisoner.

"It's a bit harsher than I'd expected, but going AWOL has been declared a prevalent offence and unfortunately the colonel has chosen to make an example of you to help deter any others in a similar frame of mind. The only thing that stopped him awarding you the 'services no longer required' tag is your previous good record and the fact that you did come back voluntarily. Do you understand that? You've been given a second chance. So don't stuff it up. Do your time, come back. Keep your nose clean and we might even still be able to get you away with the November flight."

"Yes, sah!" said the soldier, which was about as much as he was expected or allowed to say anyway.

The regimental sergeant major turned to the regimental police sergeant who'd been waiting expectantly. "Take him away, sergeant," he said. "Battalion headquarters will make the necessary arrangements, and will let you know what they are. He'll need an escort, of course."

"Yes, sah!" said the regimental police sergeant, thinking: I do know my job, sir. "Prisoner!" he barked. "Double march! Left, right, left, right, left wheel, left, right, left right, get 'em up! Get 'em up! Right wheel! Left, right, left, right."

The pair disappeared rapidly out the double doors and down the road where, once out of sight and earshot of anybody in Bullshit Castle, the sergeant slacked off the pace and they made their way back to the battalion cellblock at an easy double time.

Private John Harris gave a big sigh. The official part was all over and at least he now knew exactly what was going to happen. The biggest relief of all was that he wasn't going to be kicked out. He hadn't actually planned on going AWOL. It just sort of happened. He'd been on leave in Auckland, initially teaming up with his soldier mate Steve, who'd gone to his parents' place. But after five days of partying, drinking and carrying on like a couple of pork chops, they'd been asked to leave.

So they booked into a local pub, but Steve promptly disappeared with a solo mum he'd met. Then on the final Friday night in the bar, after a boozy two weeks, John met this gorgeous 18-year-old Maori girl. The two had hit it off straight away and she took him home with her that night to begin something of a marathon in bed.

John had been absolutely rapt. Nothing like this had ever happened to him before and he'd completely flipped, all sense and logic going out the window. He was head over heels in love, or so he thought, and it seemed far more important than getting back to the battalion on time.

He hadn't intended or even wanted to overstay his leave by nearly five weeks. But the girl, Mere, just hadn't wanted him to leave. In fact, she'd begged him not to. Then her brother got him a job at the abattoir where he was a foreman, making it even harder for John to think about returning.

It had been a grand month, though. Almost like a honeymoon, he supposed, spending most of it in bed when he wasn't at work or she on her course. But it all ended abruptly when her mother unexpectedly arrived on the doorstep from up north. She wasn't too pleased to find a pakeha sharing the same bed as the daughter for whom she had great career plans.

She blamed the brother and his wife for the carry-on, and the arguing became bitter and even nasty. Eventually John was ordered to leave. He wasn't from Auckland, he was running low on loot and he had nowhere to stay. He hung around for another week or so, trying to see Mere, but was constantly blocked by her mother. He was devastated when she disappeared. Her mother took her back up north and the brother, still smarting from her ear-bashings, wasn't too much help. He told John to disappear as well.

Broke and broken-hearted, John decided to head back to the battalion. He sadly handed himself in to the local territorial battalion, because he had no money to make his own way back to Christchurch. He soon found himself in the cells at Burnham and up on charge, copping the 60 days. To be honest, he knew he thoroughly deserved it.

With the benefit of a bit of hindsight, he realised that he and Mere probably hadn't been in love, just in lust, and it probably wouldn't have lasted anyway. At least, that's what he desperately tried to convince himself. But without too much success.

It still hurt when he thought about her. But then as far as he knew, she'd never made an attempt to contact him or even left a message. This broke his heart. With difficulty, he brought his mind back to the here and now. Some of the hardened old army vets reckoned you weren't a real soldier until you'd done time. But John knew from listening to guys who'd done their time at Ardmore that he was going to get a hard time up there.

He was determined not to let it get to him, though. He was tough, pretty fit, and knew he would just have to hang on in there and grind it out somehow. He'd heard stories about guys who'd cracked up in there. He didn't know if they were true or not, but he was a grunt and they weren't going to crack him, by God. No way.

Two days later, escorted by a regimental police lance corporal whom he knew slightly, he was flown to Whenuapai in an ancient Bristol Freighter, or 40,000 rivets flying in formation as they were known by all and sundry in the services. The prisoner and escort were met by a Land Rover and driver and swiftly transported to the Ardmore Military Prison at Clevedon.

The prison, a relic of World War II, sat on 60 acres or so of Ministry of Defence land incorporating the army's rifle range, a pine (and gorse) plantation, a tip and ammunition storage and various other storage bays, most dating back to wartime days. It was covered in scrub, gorse or trees where it wasn't maintained for shooting purposes or access.

There was a little bit of rough grazing available and some of the staff ran a steer or two. There was also a pigsty, whose occupants appeared to be doing very on the waste from the prison, thank you very much. In fact, as John was soon to discover, the pigs did far better than the prisoners. He was also to find out there was plenty of work to be done on the large, generally overgrown block of land, and the staff weren't too slow in finding chores for their prisoners.

It didn't take long for the harassment to begin. But John was surprised that the first target was the unfortunate lance corporal, who was deemed not to have acted regimentally enough when entering the prison to hand him over. He copped an earful from the master at arms, the 2IC to the prison's captain commandant and apparently the navy equivalent to an RSM. This master was already shaping up like a nasty sort, in John's mind, and the poor corporal looked extremely relieved when he finally got to get out of the joint.

Now it was John's turn. They soon had him running round the place or marking time at the double while they screamed confusing and conflicting orders at him, as an introduction to the establishment. It was all orchestrated and co-ordinated by the master himself, who very obviously considered himself the kingpin.

When John was read the pertinent prison standing orders, of which there seemed to be thousands, it soon became pretty clear he had virtually no rights and had to obey all the rules implicitly or run afoul of the hierarchy and suffer dire consequences.

He was to be referred to only as SUS (soldier under sentence) and had to double everywhere, marking time on arrival until halted or further directed what to do. All the staff were to be addressed as staff, no matter what rank, except the master at arms, who was to be called master, and the captain in command, who was to be addressed as 'sir'.

There were three stages of imprisonment. The first, which lasted for at least two weeks, was basically complete bastardization: Fourteen-hour days full of hard work in the prison grounds, the nearby rifle range or the pine plantation, with plenty of drill and PT thrown in for good measure. SUSs were also on the most basic diet to start, getting a full meal only at evenings. If you were lucky enough to last the first two weeks without being charged (an almost impossible feat), you moved on to Stage 2. This meant slightly fuller meals and a little bit more time to yourself. Stage 3 included a full diet and more privileges, and remission could be considered for model prisoners. A day or even a week of incarceration could be deducted from the sentence, although this happened only rarely.

But it all seemed a long way off to John, who was going through a sort of a culture shock and was being caught out by some of the more ambiguous commands, resulting in threats, ridicule and sarcasm being heaped upon him.

The master at arms seemed to have some sort of grudge against the army boys, especially grunts. "You horrible little grunter!" he exploded right in John's face, spraying flecks of spittle all over him. "Are those ears painted on? You'll have to do better than that, or you'll find yourself up on charge and still be here at Christmas time."

He was doubled up and down the place a few more times with contradictory orders yelled at him from all quarters before eventually and thankfully being herded indoors for the admin required for a new admission.

The signing in and all its accompanying bullshit took nearly two hours and included several questionnaires, one of which focused on his personal life and habits: How much did he drink? How did he spend his pay? How much did he save? Did he have life insurance? Did he attend church or want the padre to visit while he was incarcerated? The questions went on and on.

With a bit of a chip on his shoulder after all the harassment, John had a sudden rush of blood to the head and decided that it was all was none of their fucking business. He answered N/A to the questions about his personal life and habits. This bought the master at arms down on him with apoplectic vengeance. "Who the hell do you think you are!" he screamed. "Do you want to stay in here for the rest of the year, you young punk? That can easily be arranged! Or do you just want your head punched in?" A threatening pause. "I can do either – or both!" he screamed.

The master's raging red countenance was now right in John's face, only inches away and edging ever closer. Spittle rained all over the prisoner as he stared right back at the very upset naval warrant officer who was desperately trying to intimidate him.

A cold calm settled over John as he realised it was all on. Well come on then, you fucking old cunt, bring it on, he thought. He turned slightly sideways, cocking his fist at the same time, waiting.

His eyes must have signalled his defiance, too, because the master suddenly stopped his advance. Face ruddy, eyes popping out of their sockets, he screamed: "You! You're on charge! Insubordination! Staff!" He turned to the army sergeant who had suddenly materialised. "You're my witness. Get this insubordinate arsehole out of my sight before I do something I might regret. Take him away for a hard run through the pines. Might teach him to show a little more respect to his superiors."

John was quickly doubled away by the ageing sergeant. Like most of the prison staff, he was probably just filling in time until retiring after 20, 25 or possibly even 30 years' service.

He was directed down the road toward the range at a fast pace, although it slowed somewhat noticeably once out of sight of the prison. Eventually the sergeant ran out of breath and called a halt. After a few moments of recovery time, he spoke.

"I'm Sergeant Morris and I'll give you a little bit of good advice because you haven't made a very auspicious start here at all, have you?" he said. "The master just doesn't like army people at the best of times, and for some reason particularly has it in for the infantry. So I strongly suggest you just play along and just do what is required. Otherwise, if you get him on your back, he'll do his best to prolong your time here and make it as miserable as he can."

The sergeant was silent for a few seconds then asked: "Do you understand what I'm saying?"

"Yes, staff," snapped John.

"Good. When we get back, fill out the forms properly. You can put anything in. It doesn't even have to be the truth. Fill them out with bullshit, if you want. Remember, BBB – bullshit baffles brains. Just keep him happy, all right?"

"Yes, staff," said John.

"Good," said Sergeant Morris. "We'll head back now and you'd better be breathing heavily when we get there, or he'll think I've been giving you too easy a time. And that won't help matters at all."

John didn't have to pretend to be breathing heavily when they got back, even though he'd actually been extremely fit at the time of going AWOL. Seven weeks of drinking and no exercise except rooting had taken their toll, despite one of his fellow soldier's theories that a good root was the equivalent of a seven-mile run.

He was young, his residual fitness was very good and he had no trouble keeping up with the pace set by the ageing sergeant. Even so, he was panting by the time they got back to the prison grounds.

He filled out the forms as suggested by the sergeant, bullshitting his arse off and putting anything down. Then he was allotted his cell and issued with his prison kit, and had to make up his bedroll to exacting specifications. This all done, it was time for a shower and dinner.

The meal, concocted by a crusty old navy cook, wasn't too bad and he met his fellow inmates at the prisoners' mess. There were five other guests in residence – one navy, two air force and two army boys, one of them a Fijian infantryman doing 90 days for the dastardly crime of punching the orderly officer at Linton camp while skunk-drunk.

None had too much to say, not that they were allowed to talk to each other anyway. The Fijian maintained a huge permanent smile on his face as they all went at their food like a dog at its dinner. They'd obviously been working hard on short rations.

After dinner, they all had to help with the dishes and cleaning up, with one of the Stage 2 guys getting the cushy job of feeding the pigs. Depending on what stage they were at, they then went off to do drill, maintenance, washing and ironing, letter-writing or just reading the Bible, the only book they were issued with.

John found himself doing drill with the Fijian, who still had the smile on his face, and the two air force boys, who were each in for 30 days after the baggies' bar they were running at the air base was found to have had a rather serious shortfall in takings.

It was all reasonably easy. The master at arms and day staff had departed, thank Christ, and the two night duty staff, navy and air force respectively, were obviously just filling in time until retirement and weren't vindictive or out to prove anything. John was beginning to realise that most of the staff only acted like strict disciplinarians when the master was around. They slacked off considerably when he went home.

Finally locked in his cell for the night at 1900hrs, he had no trouble at all getting off to sleep, although he was awoken a couple of times by the night staff doing their required checks. Just making sure no one was ill or had attempted sideways, as suicide was commonly referred to in the army

The following day commenced at 0500hrs when the prisoners were rudely awakened as lights were turned on and cell doors thrown open. They were given half an hour to get their cell into inspection order before sent to the showers. Coming from a regimental environment, John didn't have any real worries with the required bedroll and layout – or so he thought – and was easily ready for the initial inspection by the night staff at 0600hrs.

Following that, they were doubled off to breakfast, which consisted only of a plate of unsweetened porridge and a cup of tea for the first stagers. Not exactly the most complete meal he had ever eaten in his life, even in the field. After mess fatigues, it was out for a bit of drill in the compound while the night staff handed over, then it was back into the cells for an inspection by the master at arms. After the previous day's performance, John should have known that his cell would be nowhere near satisfactory for this fine gentleman. Most of his stuff ended up plastered all over the floor amid more shouted threats, abuse and ridicule.

He didn't have enough time to get it right again before they were doubled out for the daily parade, inspection and drill, conducted by (no surprises for guessing) the master himself. He was obviously right in his element here, giving them all a torrid time. Lacking a regimental background and not that clever at drill, the air force and navy inmates were his particular targets. This took the heat off John, Waqa the Fijian and the other army bloke, who was due for release in a couple of days anyway.

John was ordered to have his cell back into inspection order to by lunch time, which probably wouldn't give him much time to eat. But when one of the other prisoners sniggered cynically that he wouldn't miss much anyway, he didn't feel quite so bad.

After a trying inspection and laborious drill conducted by the master, they were all glad when he finally handed over to the other day staff, an air force sergeant and a very large naval person whose rank John couldn't figure out. But they only had to call him staff, anyway.

PT was the next item on the agenda. This consisted of a warm-up then a run down to the rifle range butts and back, a distance of about a mile, followed by exercises to finish off with. It wasn't too surprising when the large navy chap drove a Land Rover down to the butts, rather than run there to check that they actually did the full distance before turning back. John easily kept up with the others on the way down. The non-army blokes, whose jobs obviously didn't include too much PT, struggled to stay with the group.

On the way back, he and the Fijian pulled away from the others without too much effort and had a bit of a sprint at the end, finishing locked together amid encouragement from the day staff and the master, who had come out to watch.

The master growled at the Fijian, saying: "I knew you were swinging the lead, Waqa. I'll expect you to try that hard all the time from now on, I'll be watching you, me lad." He stalked away. Waqa's face cracked into an even bigger grin at the departing master. It was no wonder the rest of the staff all called him Smiley.

The party was split up then, with the Stage 2 inmates given the easier work around the prison, and the rest to labour in the pine plantation, directed by a couple of the staff. John found himself paired with Smiley under the large navy chap, Staff Bowers. They were to clear scrub – mostly large gorse bushes – from between the pine trees in the plantation, and they were issued with a slasher and a pair of gloves each for hauling the prickly shit to a central point in a clearing to be burned.

Staff Bowers seemed to watch them closely for a while then obviously grew bored, switched off and sat down. Waqa then revealed a devious mind lurked behind his wide smile and open face. He showed John one of the little tricks he'd developed. "It only works for a couple of the staff," he whispered as they slashed their way into a particularly heavy patch of gorse among the trees, and cleared a small space.

Back-piling the gorse over the path they'd made, he gestured to John to sit down. Waqa sat too, but every now and again he'd bang the back of his slasher against a tree a few times, making a noise to keep up the pretence that they were working. Of course, he explained to John, you have to have something to show for the morning effort. And you have to watch out, because sometimes the master at arms shows up unexpectedly. But generally the tactic gives you a bit of a break, if you are lucky. John was quickly learning that when you're on short rations and doing hard labour, any break is a good break.

Waqa was pretty sure that Staff Bowers knew about the ploy. He usually positioned himself where he could see anyone coming towards them, and would warn them. He didn't really care what the inmates did, as long as some work got done and he didn't get into trouble himself.

Despite the short breaks, John was happy when they were finally doubled back to the prison for lunch. The unaccustomed work caused a bunch of blisters on both hands, the stinging making him feel the pinch a bit. Lunch for the first stagers consisted of a plate of soup, a couple of slices of bread minus butter, and a cup of tea, which was soon wolfed down. Then John was sent straight back to tidy his cell for the re-inspection while the others did the mess fatigues.

After what seemed like all too short a respite, it was back to the pine plantation to continue bashing and hauling scrub. Around three o'clock, John found himself being doubled back to the prison again, on his own this time, to go up on the insubordination charge the master at arms had landed him with.

He soon found the master was quite capable of embroidering the truth where it suited him, as his description of John's supposed indiscretion to the commandant was quite fanciful. John surprised the master by freely admitting the charge but saying that as a new arrival, he had been confused by all the shouting, orders and counter-orders going on and had initially thought that answering the survey was optional. The master was quite hacked off when John was awarded only three extra periods of drill. He vented his spleen when they were out of earshot of the commandant, calling John a fucking liar and threatening to get him "one way or another". John wisely said nothing and was just glad the day was Friday. Waqa had told him the weekends were generally pretty good because the master didn't usually work.

They were bought back to the prison at 1700hrs to clean up the tools and have a shower before dinner, which thankfully for all the ravenous Stage 1 inmates consisted of a full meal. After the mess fatigues, they were all given various tasks round the compound while John had one of his periods of extra drill administered by the half-hearted air force sergeant, who obviously had no real interest in it at all. All the same, he was thankful when he was finally locked in his cell at 1900hrs. It had been a long day and he was quite stuffed, with his blistered hands still stinging. He didn't even hear the first cell check that night because he was sound asleep.

The weekend was quite reasonable, considering. They were kept very busy with scrub-bashing, lawn-mowing and keeping the prison structure up to scratch. There was plenty of brass round the place, requiring constant polishing and burnishing to stay shiny. There were windows to clean, cobwebs to be done away with and sweeping and weeding to be done. There always seemed to be something requiring attention, which certainly made the days go quickly. And even if there was nothing needing to be done, they'd just be made to redo something that was already perfect anyway.

There was also the maintenance of the staff bar. The prisoners had to keep it clean and tidy and the others told John that sometimes they found cigarettes and half-empty bottles of soft drink or even beer, which they generally consumed very quickly. The risks were huge if they were caught. This job was also regarded as a bit of a perk and generally awarded to the Stage 2 or Stage 3 prisoners, not the hard doers.

It was Monday mornings that the prisoners really dreaded, and John was soon to find out why. It was the day of the commandant's barrack inspection and parade, which the master generally used as an ideal excuse to give the inmates an extra portion of arseholes. He was usually in bright and early in the morning, rousing everyone out of their cells earlier than usual and having them flying around in all directions. He had this habit of ordering them to perform a task and leaving them to do it, but then sneaking back again to try and catch them slacking off.

John found himself copying Waqa, who worked speedily enough when any of the staff were around but slowed considerably when they weren't, although never enough to be accused of slacking off. Any faults found by the commandant during the inspection were regarded as a personal insult to the master, and woe betide the prisoners whose cells or fatigues didn't come up to scratch. If he didn't actually charge them with anything, he'd certainly make sure the rest of their day was an utter and complete misery. It wasn't too long before John arrived at the same conclusion as all the other prisoners and probably most of the guards: Jesus might love the master at arms but everyone else thought he was just a cunt.

The inspection resulted in a couple of charges – none for John but one for Waqa. Then it was time for what was called the cross-country run, although this was done on the road. The air force and navy boys dreaded this event, which usually took place on Mondays and Fridays and consisted of a run around the Ardmore airfield, while still wearing boots. The course was around five and a half miles, though sometimes the master stretched it out to nearer 10 miles if he was in a particularly bad mood.

Both John and Waqa cruised it because the other service lads really dragged the chain in the rear, ensuring a slow pace. Unlike the infantrymen, they had no idea how to switch their minds off and listen to the rhythm of the boots striking the ground. Thumb up bum and mind in neutral, as one of John's platoon sergeants once said. Eventually the group was forced to walk when the weakest runner blew his arse. He was roundly and solidly abused by the master and called every sort of lazy bastard under the sun.

But it still made no difference. It seemed running was just not that particular prisoner's forte. Once they turned off the highway on to the winding road back up to the prison, the rest of them were ordered to sprint ahead while the master harangued the less fortunate one. John and Waqa were both glad that he had found someone else to pick on. But they both had to admit he was a fit old bastard.

After the run it was a shower then back to the pine plantation until lunchtime, with the rest of the afternoon spent grubbing gorse as well. The only good thing about that was they were out of the clutches of the master at arms. Apart from the odd swoop, he tended to stay back at the prison. Thank the Good Lord for that.

The next three weeks fairly sped by in a similar boring vein and before John knew it, a third of his sentence was up. The days very long, tiring and much of a muchness, while the nights seemed all too short. He was as fit as a buck rat by now, literally jumping out of his skin, with the work and PT holding no fears for him at all. In fact, he and Waqa had actually broken the record for a couple of the runs. The master was totally disgusted, saying he always knew the Fijian had been taking it easy before John arrived.

John had also managed to stay clear of any more charges, although he didn't quite know how. The master was always lurking, looking to catch him out and threatening to punch him up or worse. But he never seemed to get around to it.

Prisoners came and went, some for short sentences of only a week, some for longer. John was sorry to lose Waqa, whose time finally expired. He was shipped straight back to Fiji, no doubt in disgrace for what he'd done. The navy bloke was freed early with a bit of remission for good behaviour and could hardly wait to get out of the place, hating the regime and especially the long runs the master rejoiced in. John and the two air force boys were now on Stage 2, all as fit as they'd ever been since basics. The Brylcreem boys still detested the long runs, though.

There were four new prisoners, three army and one navy, in for various offences – theft, AWOL or plain drunken brawling. The master, who was a vindictive sort of a bastard at the best of times, particularly hated thieves. He gave a young army chap convicted of this offence a particularly hard time, saying that any soldier who'd steal off another was just scum of the earth. The prisoner was actually reduced to tears a few times. Although this took the heat off the others, they all felt sorry for this particular guy. He just couldn't cope with the strict discipline and the master's constant bullying, and he could often be heard crying mournfully in his cell at night.

Unable to do anything about Mere, John was quite settled emotionally by now. He didn't even allow himself the luxury of thinking about her. He was content to serve out his time, get back to the battalion and hopefully catch the next flight up to Asia.

He had no family or friends in Auckland, so it was a bit of a shock one Saturday morning when he was informed he had visitors. Somewhat puzzled, he was permitted to go to the lawn area at the front of the prison. To his utter astonishment, a thinner and pale-looking Mere and her brother were waiting for him. She flew into his arms and burst into tears while her brother Mark, with a wide smile on his face and not at all dismayed by the surroundings, did some explaining.

"Mum gave up," he said. "This one wouldn't eat, sleep, wouldn't do anything. She was bloody useless, eh? So I reckon you better have her." John didn't even hear the end of the story; he was too caught up with other things. He and Mere eventually managed to untangled themselves and she explained what had happened. Her Mum had made her go back up north to the family farm, way out in the sticks, hoping she would eventually forget about him.

But she hadn't. She and her mother had fought and argued until eventually her Mum, amidst tears and recriminations, had finally given in. Sadly, she told Mere that she'd wanted her to do well in life, achieving a qualification leading to a good job, and not becoming just another teenage solo mother. Mere had no way of contacting John until she got back to Auckland, where she promptly rang the army and found where he was.

Visiting time was up all too quickly, with Mere promising to come back as often as she could until he got out. He was allowed one visit a week. After the visit, John found himself in emotional turmoil again. All the feelings that he'd thought he'd gotten over came flooding back, and the month or so left of his sentence now seeming like a lifetime. He felt a sudden desperation to get out of the place.

This feeling grew worse on the following Monday when he was placed on charge by the master for what he felt was a minor, and nit-picking reason. Marched in front of the commandant to answer the charge, he made the mistake of saying what he thought, arguing that it was just plain harassment. Surprisingly, he was awarded only two extra periods of drill. This fair pissed the master off. If he wasn't on John's case before, he now solemnly promised to be so now. He angrily threatened him again, once out of sight and hearing of the commandant. John did notice, however, that he no longer got right in his face, because he knew John was not going to back down from any physical confrontation. But this was of no consolation. He just didn't want to have to put up with all the bullshit for another month. He was breaking his neck to be back with his Mere.

A new prisoner came in later that day, an overweight army driver who, like John, had been AWOL for more than a month. The master was in an extra foul mood that week, probably because of John, and hit on the guy immediately, calling him a prize porker and threatening to put him in the pigsty. It was very obvious that the poor chap was going to struggle with the regime, especially the PT, and John didn't envy him at all. For his own part, however, he concentrated on keeping his head down and staying out of the limelight. Unfortunately, the plan went awry.

The trouble started late on the Wednesday afternoon while they were up in the plantation grubbing gorse. It fair pissed down and eventually the staff doubled them back to the prison early. The master was highly critical of the staff, saying they were far too soft, and he wouldn't allow the thoroughly soaked prisoners the luxury of an immediate shower. Instead he gave them all different tasks around the prison, under his supervision while the staff showered.

John was tasked to clean and oil the tools and tidy the tool shed. This didn't take him very long because it was already pristine, and he began looking at an old newspaper he found in one of the rubbish bins. Then in bustled the master.

"You fucking idle cunt!" he screamed, closing the distance between the two so swiftly that John was taken completely by surprise when his face was slapped with a vicious back-hander. John staggered backwards with the force of the blow, which really made his head buzz for a few seconds. Then recovering his wits and quickly consumed by anger, he put his fists up. "Come on then, you fucking old cunt," he hissed.

Unfortunately the words had exploded out before he could even begin to think sensibly. For a couple of seconds the two just glared at each other. John could see the master weighing up the situation and for a moment or two he thought it was all on.

Then the master screamed: "Get back to your fucking cell now, you mutinous bastard. We'll see how smart you are in the orderly room. I've got you by the balls this time."

John's rage evaporated swiftly and he was thoroughly pissed off at the turn of events. Christ, he thought, I'd only just picked the paper up, too. Didn't even have time to read the bloody thing.

Dejectedly and disgustedly, he entered his cell and flopped down on the bare wooden slats, which was a definite no-no during the day. It was not a hell of a smart move and a few seconds later, the master entered the cell and really went off his tree, calling John every sort of cunt under the sun.

John leapt to his feet, frustration boiling over and any reason rapidly disappearing out of his head. He'd reached the end of his tether. He'd had enough. If this old cunt wanted a go, he could fucking well have one. Leering at the master with a vicious grin on his face, he gestured with his hands. "Come on, come on, ya big brave bully man. Let's be having ya, then."

The master stood stock still, anchored solidly at the door. Something was wrong. Somehow he couldn't intimidate this particular prisoner, who acted as if he didn't give a stuff, and was even inviting him to have a go. It was as far outside normal inmate behaviour as he'd ever experienced. Being a big man and a sadistic bully, he was accustomed to always getting his own way. It stabbed his considerable ego that this fucking army bastard – infantry, to make it worse – was standing up to him. The prisoner was not only standing his ground, but also blatantly inviting him to have a go.

The master didn't like it at all. Nor did he like the contemptuous look in the prisoner's eyes. He desperately wanted to knock that look out of those eyes. But he couldn't move. He remained stationary at the door, his mind absolutely refusing to tell his legs to move. The two glared viciously at each other for what seemed like at least five minutes but was probably only one at the most.

Finally the master managed to croak: "Staff." Louder a second time: "Staff!" One of the navy chaps quickly materialised. He obviously had been lurking not too far away and had probably overheard everything.

"This prisoner is on two charges," the master said. "Insubordination, and threatening a superior officer. These are serious charges, so I'll leave you here to you here to carry on while I organise things. The prisoner is confined to his cell in the meantime."

"Yes, sir," the navy man said briskly. With a final venomous glare at John, the master departed. The navy man looked at John with what seemed like sympathetic eyes, shaking his head sadly before slowly pulling the door to with a final and empty-sounding clunk.

Not giving a regimental fuck about prison rules now, John shrank down to the wooden slats with a sense of depression enveloping him. I've really done it this time, he thought. I'll never get out of the bloody joint, not with that bullying cunt constantly picking on me.

Freedom and Mere seemed further and further away. John was thrust into despair.

He surprised the commandant and especially the master by not bothering to defend the charges. He just said if the master declared he was guilty, then he must be, although he couldn't really recall committing the offences. Asked how he got the swollen face, John felt like saying: "Ask the master." But, with a very contemptuous look on his face, he merely replied that he'd been accidentally back-swiped by a branch while working in the plantation.

The commandant didn't dwell too much on the case before sentencing John to loss of remission on the charge of insubordination and seven days' extra on his sentence for threatening a superior officer. After a stirring lecture about discipline, he was double marched out of the room and handed straight over to one of the other staff, with the master having been ordered to come back in to talk to the commandant. He rejoined the other prisoners up at the plantation with a gathering sense of hopelessness and a sharp pain in his heart. He didn't recognise the symptoms for what they were – a genuine case of love-sickness.

As the next few days straggled by, the master seemed avoid John and left him to be supervised by the other staff. John wondered if the commandant had been asking questions about the state of the prisoner's face. Whatever the case, he was grateful for the respite. But he wasn't so pleased when informed that because of the charges he was also back on Stage 1, and even more devastated when told he would no longer be allowed visitors. This was a crushing blow, another demonstration of the master's vindictiveness.

That night, alone in his cell, he felt a desperate need to get out. Instead, he'd been awarded extra time and had every likelihood of accumulating more, the way things were going. He shook himself mentally, realising he was in danger of wallowing in self-pity. His fighting spirit returned. "I won't let that old cunt beat me," he said aloud to the cell door. "I won't let that old cunt beat me."

The master called an O Group of all staff early the next morning, before the commandant came in and the night shift went home. "No doubt you would have all heard that I have had an open challenge to my authority by SUS Harris," he said. "He has been awarded seven extra days' confinement, which I consider a very light punishment for the offence. Any challenge to any of the staff's authority will not be tolerated and should be quickly reported and the culprit disciplined. Do you all understand?"

He glared at the staff, almost all of whom were probably thinking: "You're the only one who has had any problem." No one said anything, however, and the master continued: "I want SUS Harris supervised very closely. He has a huge chip on his shoulder and if he shows any further sign of rebellion or even resentment, I am to be informed immediately and he will be charged ASAP."

There were a few moments of silence as he looked over each of his staff individually. "All right," he said. "Dismissed. Don't forget what I have just told you." The day staff went about their duties and the night staff home to sleep, each with his own thoughts about the master's so-called discipline problem.

That evening the army sergeant on the night shift had a quiet word with John, warning him that the master seemed to be out to get him and advising him to keep a low profile. John thanked him for the tip, although it was nothing he hadn't already worked out for himself anyway.

His prediction about the fat driver struggling with the prison regime, especially PT, proved to be spot on. When all the prisoners went for a regular run round the Ardmore aerodrome – only the short version of around five and a half miles – the driver eventually collapsed after having been harassed and abused most of the way for not keeping up. He had actually been trying to stop from about the three-mile point onwards. But the master wouldn't let him, and kept pushing him back into the line and making him run on.

John bit his tongue for a long time but eventually couldn't help himself and burst out: "Can't you see he's had enough, master? Why don't you leave him alone?"

The master stopped the squad with a victorious look in his eye. "I've got you again, Harris!" he exploded. "You're on charge. When I need advice from the likes of you, I'll ask for it." He just couldn't stop himself, adding: "Keep it up and you could be here until Christmas, the way you're going!"

At least there were no physical threats this time, perhaps because they were away from the prison and instant back-up. But still, John's heart sank. Freedom seemed to be getting further and further away.

The squad ran on until they were about a mile from the prison, when the big driver finally keeled over, almost delirious and frothing at the mouth. He wasn't looking or sounding that good and, belatedly, the master became quite concerned. He brusquely ordered John, one of the fittest of the prisoners, to double back to the prison and get one of the staff to bring the quarter-ton Land Rover to pick up the casualty.

On arrival back at the prison, John had trouble finding even one of the staff, as they tended to slack off and disappear when the master and the prisoners weren't there, especially those who lived in the small housing area attached to the complex.

The Land Rover was parked right out the front and he easily found the keys and the RIs in the office. He was just considering whether or not to drive the Rover himself when one of the navy chaps finally put in an appearance. John quickly explained the situation, and accompanied the staff member as the pick-up was made and the semi-conscious driver taken straight to the Papakura military camp hospital, where he was kept in overnight for observation.

Afterwards, while the master doubled the rest of them back to the prison, the germ of an idea occurred to John. The big army driver was back by lunchtime the next day and placed on light duties for two days. This really enraged the master, who roared that it was a prison for the punishment of soldiers and not a fucking holiday camp.

Still, it kept some of the heat off the rest of the prisoners for the next couple of days as the master spent his time trying to devise ways of keeping the fat driver active and busy round the place. The poor chap would probably have nightmares about the vindictive bastard for the rest of his life, John thought. Sadly, the couple of days on so-called light duties passed all too quickly for the driver and he soon found himself back in the swim with the rest of them.

John went up on the charge and found himself with another three days added to his sentence, plus a stern warning that if he fronted up again he would be most severely dealt with. Absolutely no mention was made of the fate that had befallen the fat driver or what John's comments had referred to.

That night in his cell, he had a real attack of the miseries, knowing the master had it in for him and despairing that he would ever get out of the place. He was finding it harder and harder to keep his chin up and persevere, with all the bullshit coming his way

When the master announced they were going to run the 10-mile circuit on the following Friday, John's ears pricked up. He was determined to get out of the place somehow and this could just be his opportunity. He knew the master would pick on the fat boy, who would almost certainly blow his arse again. It was odds-on that easily being the fittest of the prisoners, he'd be the one asked to run back to get assistance. If no one was about when he got back, he might be able to get access to vehicle keys.

There were a lot of ifs but John had had a gutsful. He was prepared to throw caution to the wind because he could just see himself assaulting the master if he stayed much longer and he had an urgent craving to be with his woman. He was prepared to take the risk if the opportunity arose.

It was a hot day, much hotter than the previous time when the driver had blown it, and it became obvious the master had learned nothing, because he soon had them running along at a very smart clip. They hadn't even got halfway before the distress signals were obvious and the driver broke step, trying to escape the middle of the small group where he'd been deliberately placed in an attempt to make him keep up.

He copped an earful, was pushed roughly back into line, and the pace slackened a touch. This tactic worked for another mile or so, but the driver was soon out of step and stumbling again, upsetting the rhythm of the group. The master halted them and hooked into the unfortunate driver, who tried to lie down on the side of the road but was hauled unceremoniously back to his feet.

"You're not going to pull the wool again, boy!" the master screamed. "Get back into the fucking line, you lazy, fat slob!" He placed the heaving driver at the front of the group this time and off they set at an even slower pace. Twice more the driver went down; twice more he was hauled roughly to his feet and made to continue. He began to froth at the mouth again, staggering and reeling with every step. He also seemed a bit delirious, just like the previous time.

John realised it couldn't go on. He almost said something again, but he knew that would probably only make the master even more determined. So he held his tongue, although he could hear muttering from several other prisoners. Somehow the driver made another half mile before going down for the final count, still about three miles from the compound. The others gathered round as the master tried unsuccessfully to rouse the unfortunate victim. But he was absolutely comatose by now, face red as a beetroot, hot as hell and panting for breath.

John had served in Asia with the battalion and had seen soldiers with both heat exhaustion and the rather more dangerous next stage, heat stroke. He noticed the victim had virtually stopped sweating, a classic symptom of the latter condition. He was concerned enough to speak up again, but suddenly the master began giving orders.

"SUS Harris!" he roared. "Get yourself back to the prison and tell one of the staff to bring the Land Rover down. I don't like the look of him. He's too hot. Tell whoever brings the Rover we'll be over at the river trying to cool him down. You can get the vehicle through the gate here. Off you go." John doubled away as the master ordered the rest of the prisoners to pick up the victim. That was a good move. Cold water, especially on his head, should soon bring the poor bugger right. John shook his head ruefully. God, that master was a dumb cunt though, he thought. The silly old prick had never learned a thing from the first time it had happened. He'd probably kill someone one day. John put a spurt on, never ever dreaming how prophetic his thoughts were.

After at least four miles of very conflicting thoughts, he found himself galloping up the hill toward the prison with a big decision to make. As he had expected for a Friday afternoon, the place looked deserted. The quarter-tonner was parked right out the front. John looked around. He couldn't see a soul, so he entered the main door and headed for the office. It was just as deserted inside as out. From away down the corridor, he could just hear the muted hum of a radio and the bash of a pan or perhaps a cupboard closing. The old hash-slinger was preparing dinner.

The RIs and keys were in their normal place, so he took them and headed back down the corridor. He realised he was probably very vulnerable right now if caught, so he called out, not too loudly though: "Hello, hello."

Nothing stirred. His voice echoed in the empty corridor. He continued on out the door and headed for the Rover. Serious decision time. He could either take the Rover down to pick up his fellow prisoner, or he could do a runner. He sat in the Rover thinking how much he hated the place, how much he hated the master at arms, and how much he wanted to be with Mere. If he did drive the vehicle down and pick up the prisoner himself, the master wouldn't be happy. He'd probably charge him with driving the vehicle unlawfully, or something stupid like that. John just hated that prick.

He looked around. Still no movement anywhere. Almost involuntarily, he turned the ignition key. The motor caught straight away and the vehicle headed off down the hill. While SUS Harris fought with his own will all the way down the hill, he never thought his decision would affect anyone except himself and Mere. He loved Mere; he hated the master at arms. If he turned right at the bottom, it would be to pick up the prisoner and finish his sentence. If he turned left, it was freedom and Mere. At the bottom of the hill the vehicle turned left and headed towards Auckland. The prisoner was on the run.

After waiting for more than an hour, with the unconscious prisoner becoming worse even though they were cooling him down in the river, the master became more and more agitated. Eventually he dispatched another prisoner to the nearest farm house to ring an ambulance. After almost another hour, it finally arrived. The ambulance officers quickly recognised the patient's serious condition and with lights flashing and siren screaming, departed for Middlemore Hospital.

The master, perhaps a little perturbed by now but still furious at the non-arrival of the Rover, began to double the rest of the prisoners back to the compound. They were met by one of the staff who had finally become concerned by the non-appearance of the runners. With no Rover available, he drove his own car out to check. The prisoners were literally thrown into the back of the vehicle and driven back to the compound, where they were put straight into their cells.

The Rover was gone. None of the staff had it. SUS Harris had disappeared. The master found himself having to ring the commandant with the sorry tale. There was no happy hour that night in the staff bar. Regimental Number 684441 Driver Leon Short passed away later that evening, his heart having given up the ghost.

Regimental Number 844562 Private John Harris was posted as having escaped from Ardmore Prison. The Land Rover was found abandoned at Mangere airport the following Tuesday. The army still had John's passport. But back then, you didn't need one to go to Australia.

A subsequent check of passenger lists failed to reveal either his or Mere's names. Inquiries among the Maori community revealed nothing. The MOD conducted a closed Board of Inquiry into both incidents, interviewing the rest of the prisoners. They all detested the master and didn't pull any punches. They recounted that that the driver had collapsed on a previous occasion when forced to continue running by the master, and had spent the night in Papakura camp hospital. One of them said John had told him that the swelling on his face had come from a blow by the master. Of course, the commandant had told the board that he had asked the master about the prisoner's swollen face and he had seemingly lied about it.

The master tried to blame the death on the escaped prisoner, saying he had ordered him to get assistance. But he failed to convince the board, who told him he had been in charge and obviously hadn't learned from a previous similar occasion. The master was found culpable in both incidents and relieved of his position with a considerable loss of seniority, and forced into retirement.

Not a hell of a great punishment, you might well think, for being largely responsible for the loss of a human life. Or was it a case of the services looking after their own?

A subsequent inquiry into the way the prison system operated was also announced, which eventually resulted in the prisoners receiving full meals in recognition of the amount of physical work they were doing. The MOD released a well-watered-down version of events to the ever-curious news media, which got them off the services' back somewhat for the time being anyway. This did nothing, however, to assuage the grief and suspicions of the family of the dead soldier. They continued to ask pertinent and embarrassing questions, but got little satisfaction.

All the prisoners who had taken part in the run were given early release and forbidden to discuss the incident, especially with relatives of the dead soldier or with the press.

And John and Mere? Well, they could be in Australia or they could still be up north somewhere. Actually, they could be anywhere. Who knows? Wherever they are, let's hope they're happy, anyway.

And could anyone blame John for the death of the driver? If he had even remotely believed that the poor soldier's life was in danger, do you think he would have done things any differently? Or would his hatred of the prison and the master at arms, plus his love of Mere, still have led him to flee? Well, that will remain a regimental mystery until somebody catches up with him to ask the question. It's not even known if he is aware of the death of the driver. Somebody, somewhere must know where John is. But they ain't sayin' nothing.

WHAT THE BLOODY HELL
HAVE I GOT MYSELF INTO?

In memory of Gary Paul Ratana
14/2/1955 – 17/2/2012
RNZIR NZSAS
RIP, Rat

"On the road, three ranks, at the double – now!" The scream shattered the silence even as the light suddenly invaded the darkness.

"Move out! Move out! Come on, you lazy bastards, shake a bloody leg!" A lower, flatter voice with yet another command.

"Well, all you wannabes, it's your last chance. Do you wanna be TCs or do you wanna be sorry? Don't say we didn't warn you or give you a chance to pull out." This voice quieter and much, much more cynical. "Speak up before it's too late."

The resident comedian, as the tall, slender Maori full corporal had come to be known, was also there, the inevitable grin on his face and, as always, his demeanour different from that of his colleagues. He was strutting in a ludicrous sort of goosestep way, yelling, "Raus! Raus! Schnell! Schnell!" He must have reading Second World War comics.

The four cadre staff had snuck into the old, cold and dilapidated barracks, itself a relic from the Second World War, just before 0200hrs without anyone inside hearing a thing.

Despite being warned to be ready for anything from midnight onwards, most of them had nodded off, albeit in their clothes. Now, still half asleep, they were being energetically harried outside. They had learnt already that the most favoured punishment was press-ups on the knuckles. This morning again, these were being dished out for any misdemeanour, real or imagined.

As for the unfortunate stragglers – and there always had to be one or two – not only did they get the press-ups, but they also had to avoid the odd size-10-or-so army boot aimed loosely at their posteriors, which soon had them skittering out the door.

Eventually they were all assembled on the road in the desired formation. A search began. Three of the staff took a rank each and, using a torch, body-searched each candidate thoroughly, then expertly stripped his gear as well. Not that they had been issued that much to begin with anyway, especially in the way of creature comforts: A pack, a spare set of clothes, normal webbing, rifle and accessories, map-reading gear and a tatty grey army blanket was about their lot. The last item probably wouldn't even keep a cockroach warm and replaced the comparatively much warmer normal army sleeping bag they had been allowed on the pre-selection course.

Food-wise, they'd been issued a packet of hexamine plus cooker, and one freeze-dry meal. This was to be eaten only in emergency or when instructed, and had to be accounted for constantly. This had made it rather obvious that nutrition wasn't going feature greatly in their endeavours over the next week or so. "Christ, not even enough to keep a bloody mosquito alive," one of the guys had commented disgustedly.

While the search was being conducted, the fourth member of the staff stood back and with an eagle eye, made sure no one tried to ditch anything in the semi-darkness.

The press-up awards started again as contraband was discovered, mostly chocolate and biscuits but also some money. Several hopefuls were nabbed trying to discard theirs discreetly before being searched. But it had been stupid trying to hide perks. The staff had gleefully stripped and searched everything and had found it all. About the only place not searched was the arsehole, and who'd want to eat anything that had been lurking up there, anyway?

After all the press-ups were done, they were given a few minutes to frantically reassemble their webbing and repack their packs, the staff deliberately not letting anyone start doing this until all the searching was complete. Minutes later, finished or not and accompanied by a continual and impressive string of oaths, they were herded off down the road in a sort of un-coordinated, out-of-step gaggle, with more than a few still desperately trying to make the necessary adjustments to their gear on the run.

Something every soldier very quickly learned from bitter experience was that your gear just had to fit right and be comfortable, or you'd almost inevitably get a sore back, be chaffed to buggery, or both. But not one of them could really complain this morning. They'd all been well forewarned what it was like and no one had really expected it to be easy anyway. After all they were all volunteers and they were all stupid enough to want to attempt the NZ SAS selection course.

Lance-Corporal Pete Barron heaved a sigh of relief as the group moved off, although this was accompanied by a certain amount of trepidation, a fear of the unknown, because of the reputation the course had throughout the army and even in civvy street. But at least the long-awaited moment of truth had arrived. This after an eye-opening and strenuous month-long pre-selection course that had seen the number of candidates fall from 56 to 42.

Given the role of the SAS, it was no surprise the pre-selection had focused on the successful completion of a parachute course, physical fitness and map-reading skills, with a little bit of medical and other rougher stuff thrown in, such boxing and unarmed combat. They had learned much about themselves during that time and covered a lot of ground – a great deal more than most of them were used to – in both open and close country, by day and night. During the map-reading tasks, there always seemed to be just enough distance between the checkpoints to allow candidates to go well astray if they had made a mistake in their initial plotting, drifted off their compass bearing or misread the lay of the land.

Time constraints had also begun to be thrown in towards the end as well, just to complicate things and add that little bit more pressure. Surprisingly, this and not the para course had actually been the main reason for the pull-outs thus far, especially by the non-infantry types not too familiar with a map or the strength-sapping forced marching required to complete such an exercise without becoming geographically embarrassed, as getting lost was diplomatically termed. Several had lost just too much time and, try as they might, had simply been unable to make it up.

Although no one had actually been forced out during the pre-selection course, as would happen once the course proper started, some had pulled out because they realised they just weren't up to it, at that stage of their careers anyway. There was the wear and tear from what they were doing, the constant movement producing cuts, scrapes, bruises and falls plus one serious break, among various other minor ailments and injuries. These gave some an opportunity to withdraw on medical grounds, with at least some honour intact.

Several of the candidates, even some of the battalion boys who should really have known better, had also made the mistake of wearing boots that were not properly broken in. Of course, it didn't take too long for the grunt's enemy, blisters, to rear their ugly heads. With all the walking, running, crossing and re-crossing of rivers they were doing, causing feet to be constantly damp and allowing no healing time, these continually caused much discomfort. It's really hard to concentrate when you're walking on feet that look and feel like two great plates of raw meat. Pete had been there and made those mistakes himself in the past but so far he was holding his own, in that department anyway, touch wood.

Another unusual event that had occurred on the pre-selection was a one-on-one interview with a female civilian shrink. Pete hadn't really enjoyed that, especially all the personal questions she'd asked. He had treated it more like an interrogation and given little away, much to her evident displeasure.

He knew her report on his chances of succeeding hadn't been that optimistic but he was determined to prove her wrong. "Anyway, what the hell would a civvy know what went on in the army?" he'd indignantly asked his mate Jack afterwards. In all truth he wouldn't have even considered doing the selection course if it hadn't been for the 2IC of their company in Singapore, Captain Murray. He'd suggested it during the latter part of their second year there, when it was time to indicate where they wanted to be posted on RTNZ.

Pete had never actually enjoyed being a camp soldier. He'd never appreciated the regimental bullshit he knew he'd have to put up with if he stayed in and did the required, lengthy and mostly boring promotion courses at the School of Infantry in Waiouru. Most of the boys regarded the instructors at the "school of feet" as plastic camp soldiers with shiny boots and sharp creases.

Pete, who'd fought in Vietnam, had even found the two-year posting to Singapore quite boring at times. There had been the rugged and keenly fought inter-company rugby competition to distract them. That was almost like a minor war in itself and their company had won the symbol of supremacy, the Charlie Saxton All Black jersey, both years running. He'd also won selection for the battalion team, which was both an honour and a bit of a perk, allowing plenty of time off for training and matches.

But in general, with no war, he and several other experienced soldiers had found it very humdrum. So much so, in fact, that he'd had got into an odd spot of bother on the booze a time or two, even going as far as losing his hook for a while.

When he'd got it back the second time, he'd been given a final warning: Set a better example for the troops you're supposed to be a leader of, or else. Taking this on board and in an endeavour to keep out of the NAAFI where his troubles generally began, he'd started running of an evening after duty, eventually building up to quite an impressive mileage. Out on the road he'd begun to encounter Captain Murray and soon the two began to run together regularly.

When he'd told the Captain that he was probably going to take his discharge on RTNZ, and why, the 2IC had fair got stuck into him: Called him a bloody waster for throwing a good career away and what would he do if he got out, anyway? New Zealand wasn't exactly a land of opportunity for an ex-soldier, there's not many jobs around for retired killers, blah, blah, blah.

Then he'd surprised the hell out of Pete by suggesting he have a go at the SAS selection course. Initially Pete demurred, saying he didn't think he was good enough. But the captain persisted and after eventually extracting a somewhat reluctant yes, he speedily completed the required paperwork before any mind-change could even be contemplated.

By the time RTNZ came around, seven more Captain Murray-inspired recruits were in the team alongside Pete. Most if not all of them were probably a bit like him and wondering: "What the bloody hell have I got myself into?" It had actually been a real culture shock when, after a couple of weeks' leave, they'd all reported to the SAS

HQ. Apart from all the physical work and exercise they suddenly found were doing, they also weren't allowed to march or walk anywhere the in camp while wearing uniform. Instead, they had to double everywhere. This had proved to be a fair pain in the arse at times, but they soon learned it wasn't worth the extra attention they got if they didn't comply. They'd been constantly warned from the time they arrived: "Just remember you are being observed at all times, so don't let your standards slip."

Pete was still going over the journey to this point when a sudden, bellowed command caught all of them by surprise. "Halt!" The still-very-untidy, spread-out mob of hopefuls lurched to a thankful, panting stop. Not surprisingly, they were next to the first obstacle of the concourse.

It was now getting on towards 0400hrs on a fine but very cool morning in early May – not too far off a frost, by the feel of it. They were well away from any lights. It was as black as an ex-mother-in-law's heart. More staff were waiting, each armed with a torch, and they quickly spread out around the various obstacles of the concourse while another gave the candidates their instructions for the opening activity.

The orders were simple: Get around the concourse as quickly and safely as possible, working as a team where necessary. If you're overtaken by the two similarly clad staff setting off a few minutes behind you, you'll be automatically withdrawn. If anyone hadn't realised it was all serious stuff from here on in, they did now. No beg-your-pardons, no second chances. Fail to meet a deadline, kiddo, and you're a goner.

Pete thought fleetingly about Captain Murray's advice to him just as they left Singapore. What was it again? "Keep your head down, your mouth shut, do what's asked and try and not be noticed. Always finish with the group if you can, because if you finish first all the time you'll be noticed and given more work. And if you finish last, you'll definitely be noticed, picked on and probably forced to withdraw eventually." In infantry parlance, this was known as the thumb-in-bum and mind-in-neutral mentality. It sounded like good sense.

As they were given the command to go, he instinctively looked for his mate, big Jack Mann. He located Jack quickly in the dark, because of his distinctive height and size, and quickly closed alongside him. These two went back a long way. They did National Service together and joined RF together, went to Vietnam with the same company and shared the two-year posting to Singapore in the same company as well.

Jack had proved to be an excellent field soldier. He was as strong as an ox, and therefore a backbone for any team activity. And because of his bush upbringing, he was an outstanding map-reader and a gifted tracker, skills well appreciated by the various bosses he had served under. He was a rank ahead of Pete, having managed to keep his nose clean while Pete was fucking up in Singapore. But they were great mates and had learned to rely on and trust each other implicitly, especially in the field.

They both paced themselves, making sure to stay in the middle of the pack, and did it easily in the dark, Jack throwing or lifting Pete up on to or over any of the higher obstacles then being assisted up himself. It was all technique and teamwork, which these two rather more experienced soldiers than most on the course had down to a fine art. There were at least 15 to 20 others ahead of them by the time they finished and true to the captain's words, these early finishers were been made to double mark time while they waited for the rest.

The course was soon doubled away from the activity, with the numbers already reduced to 39. Two candidates had been overtaken by the staff members and were automatically withdrawn. Another had injured himself in a fall and was on his way to the camp hospital by Land Rover. The survivors were harassed around the camp at a breakneck speed for the next half-hour or so until stragglers gradually began to fall off the end of the formation. Finally and mercifully, they were halted outside the SAS headquarters and brusquely ordered to file into the classroom.

Here, the still-heaving candidates had to sit yet more timed psych and map-reading theory tests and buddy ratings, which Pete found quite hard because, apart from his mates from Singapore, he didn't really know many of the others that well as yet. There were just too many of them. This activity took up nearly two hours while it slowly grew lighter outside, following which they were doubled round to the side road running past the camp.

On arrival they were informed they had to do an RFL, the army's fitness-gauging run and exercises. Times and numbers were supposed to be linked to your age, but of course the SAS didn't give a hoot about your age. You were just expected to do the best you could. Leaving packs, webbing and rifles in a tidy line, they set off round the two-mile circuit still wearing boots. No one dared point out that the test was actually supposed to be completed in running shoes and not boots. Obviously, the SAS also didn't bother about minor details like that. Again, they were warned not to be overtaken by several of the staff who would set off a few minutes behind them. And again, Pete and Jack paced themselves to ensure they finished right in the middle of the pack.

The run and exercises complete with no more withdrawals, they were doubled back to the barracks. There, much to their surprise, they were ordered to go and have a shower. But there was a catch – the order wasn't made just out of the goodness of the staff's hearts.

The candidates soon discovered that sometime during the previous day, the power to the hot water cylinder had been turned off and the water was now fucking freezing on what was still a very cold morning. With several of the staff observing, most of the guys opted to have a very brief and cold sparrow's bath, accompanied by much whooping and laughing. However four "clever" guys unwisely decided to pass on the wash. They just had a cold shave and got dressed again.

When everyone was ready to go again, the non-showered ones were called out and forced to take a shower with their clothes on, accompanied by much mirth from the ones who'd braved the water. Immediately those guys were totally soaked through, the whole course was ordered to form up on the road again and doubled away, the four unfortunates still streaming water. This time it was to the Thousand Man Mess, where a special row of tables had been reserved for them, right up the front where everyone could see. After leaving packs, webbing and rifles lined tidily outside, they filed through the servery and to be presented with heaped plates of bacon, eggs, sausages, black pudding, spaghetti and baked beans – whether they wanted it or not.

As they sat down at the reserved tables, they were told by the staff already tucking in heartily at an adjacent table not to begin until everybody on the course was seated and grace had been said. When the last of the candidates sat down with his meal, the smiling comedian made them stand while he solemnly said the grace, at the completion of which he ordered them to sit.

As they reached for their knives and forks, however, he immediately screamed the command: "Out on the road! Three ranks! Now! Go! Go!" Of course, as they scattered frantically for the door, everyone else in the mess burst out laughing and shaking their heads wisely. There was an unwritten law in the army: Never volunteer for anything.

Once outside, it was straight onto the back of two RLs that had arrived, back covers drawn down so they couldn't see where they were going, and off they went, the 39 hopefuls, none really knowing what was to transpire over the next 10 days.

Pete and Jack had managed to get on to the same truck and compared notes. So far it had been nothing much, just a bit of bastardization. But there was a long way to go. They both settled down and tried to doze off. Another unwritten infantry rule: If you're not doing anything, have a gonk. You never know when you'll get another opportunity.

Just over two hours later, the trucks stopped and they were all brusquely ordered out and speedily doubled a couple of miles, downhill mostly, on a rough, gravel road lined with trees. Although most of them didn't know it yet, they were at Woodhill State Forest, a long, coast-hugging pine plantation just north of Auckland.

Eventually they halted in a clearing, where they were issued maps and briefed on the next activity. It was to be a straight-out endurance march cum map-reading exercise. They had 30 hours to complete a circuit of 50-odd miles, passing through five checkpoints on the way. These, they were to discover, were almost all cunningly placed at the top of some of the very steep knolls dotting the otherwise generally flat to gently undulating terrain.

They would be dropped off in groups of two up and down the long north-and-south-running gravel access roads on both the sea and landward side of the forest, and given the grid reference for their first checkpoint only. Of course, each of the two-man groups had a different checkpoint to aim for. It would be all too easy and pally for them to be able to walk along together.

After an abrupt "any questions?" query, to which they were given virtually no time to respond, they were all issued with their first grid reference and ordered back on to whatever truck that was taking them to their respective drop-off points. They were all too soon to find out that the hard part had only just begun.

Some six hours later found Pete head down and arse up, honking along the road. The map reading was piss-easy. He was generally heading north because he been dropped off at the southern end of the forest and there were interlinking crossroads every click or so that were clearly marked on the map. It was just a matter of counting how many you needed to cross before you got near your checkpoint – a handy guide, especially navigating without a torch in the dark, which it was by now.

The problem was the walking itself. The roads were heavily gravelled so the footing was never quite level or stable. After a while his feet, already somewhat tender from the pre-selection course, became first uncomfortable then eventually downright sore. In normal circumstances, during the day anyway, he would have walked through the trees, the soft coating of fallen pine needles cushioning his footfall. But with the distance he had to cover, he'd quickly found that this was far too slow and he had soon reverted to the road.

It was real thumb-up-bum and mind-in-neutral stuff, all right, although he had to keep a wary eye out just in case trackers were on his tail. He didn't think they would be, given the endurance-type nature of the task, but he'd found you could never be too sure with the SAS boys. They were tricky bastards.

So far he'd made only one checkpoint, where he'd been roundly abused for being so slow, made to prove he hadn't already eaten his ration, given his new grid reference on a scrap of paper and told to get on with it. He'd only just managed to find the location of the next checkpoint on the map by the light from the Tilley lamp when they kicked him out of it.

Bloody hard, he thought, and set off again, trying not to think of the constant nagging now coming from the bottom of his feet. At least it wasn't blisters, though. That would probably spell the end of his chances. He was also a bit concerned about having reached only one checkpoint so far, but little did he know that he was actually doing quite well. Only half a dozen of the others had made a checkpoint thus far, one being his mate Jack. Two others had pulled out by this time, the rolling gravel road beneath resident blisters taking its toll.

Jack, meanwhile, was doing damn fine. Being a taller man with a longer stride than most and, as he said, having harder feet from not having shoes to wear to school as a kid, the gravel didn't seem to affect him quite so much. He was fair chewing up the clicks, having also been told he was too bloody slow. But he knew that there weren't too many that could foot it with him on a route march, so he had taken it with a grain of salt and determinedly carried on.

The hours passed quickly, as they tend to do when you're busy or drinking beer, and it didn't seem very long before dawn began to lighten the eastern sky. Jack had already departed his third checkpoint and was off to the fourth, while Pete was rapidly closing into his third. Both had passed many of the others during the night, some surprisingly going the same way and to the same checkpoint, having started quite a few clicks ahead of them, but struggling and not travelling anywhere near as fast.

Others they met coming from the opposite direction gave them valuable info on where and how far they still had to go to the next checkpoint, which was really encouraging and helpful. Several had still made only one checkpoint thus far and Jack had even found one chap sound asleep at the side of the road. He thought about waking him up but decided against it. They all knew well enough what was at stake.

At each checkpoint Pete and Jack had reached, they'd found at least one person who'd pulled out of their own accord, generally because of blisters or some other medical reason.

The bottom of Pete's feet felt like parched leather but had gone totally numb by now, which was a blessed relief as far as he was concerned. He was feeling a mite hungry with all the continuous physical activity and badly felt the need of an injection of energy. They all did. It had been a long and active day and night with nary a bite to eat. This went right against that old but still oft-repeated army adage: If you don't eat you don't shit, and if you don't shit you die. But as they were beginning to discover, the SAS weren't really like the rest of the army. They were all fucking mad.

Pete was in and out of his third checkpoint very quickly. Two pull-outs were sitting quietly and sheepishly at the back but he wasn't allowed to talk to them. That made at least five withdrawals that he knew of. He already knew where the fourth checkpoint was, having been told by the guys he'd passed. But of course he didn't tell the staff. He just did a quick map check, then off again.

After a scramble down the steep knoll, he walked north-west through the pines to get to the coastal north-south road, which was decidedly flatter and made easier walking. Approaching a slightly overgrown clearing, where they had obviously loaded logs on to trucks in the past, he heard a vehicle coming up the track. Fearing discovery by SAS trackers, he concealed himself further back among the pines. But he needn't have worried. A once-white ute appeared and stopped in the clearing. Two men, obviously forestry workers, got out. One was carrying a large Thermos and they sat on a log, poured two mugs of something steaming hot and began drinking, talking and smoking. Pete watched them for a few minutes, salivating. He'd had nothing but water for almost two days. After a quick check around the area, because they'd been sternly warned against approaching the public, he decided "fuck it" and moved towards them.

"Gidday," he said as they looked up from their conversation. "Ya couldn't spare a cup of that tea, could ya mate?" He could smell it now.

"Sure, why not," one of them replied. He emptied the dregs from his mug with a backhand flick, refilled it and handed it over. "What are all you mad bastards in black doing? I saw a couple more on the road last night just before I knocked off."

Pete hesitated momentarily, then realizing he'd already broken the rules anyway, told them. He drained the tea greedily, finding it was heavily sugared at the bottom. You fuckin' beauty, he thought.

"Jesus," one of them said. "Ya must hungry, then."

"Fuckin' oath mate," replied Pete, "I could eat a horse."

While one refilled the tea mug for him, the other went to the ute, rustled around inside the cab, came up with a brown paper bag and handed it to Pete. Four corned beef sandwiches.

Pete took two, wolfed them straight down, poured the tea down his gullet, then dealt to the other two. They barely touched the sides. Finally, and feeling a bit embarrassed, he thanked them profusely.

The two forestry workers looked at each other mutely then the second one got up went to the ute, got what was probably his lunch and handed it over. Pete tried to refuse but they insisted, "Go on, ya mad bastard," one of them said. "You need it more than us. And anyway, we've got a couple a tins of meat we can heat up later if we need to."

Thanking them again, he asked them to pretend they hadn't seen him and moved off.

"Mum's the word!" one yelled as Pete waved his hand in thanks and disappeared among the trees.

He didn't go far, though. As soon as he was out of their sight, he sat down in a thicker clump of pines and scoffed his booty. It was a much-needed energy boost. And with a bit of food in his guts, he felt much better about the challenge he was facing. Five minutes later, after having concealed the evidence carefully under the pine needles, he moved off again with renewed vigour and determination.

Although he was still tired, the unexpected meal gave him energy to push himself onwards, observing the normal infantry break of 10 minutes every hour. Anymore and he might drop off to sleep, he decided. Picking up the fourth checkpoint around 1130hrs, he was more than happy to find it was only four clicks to the fifth and last one, an easy walk in comparison with some of the earlier ones. But when he got to that one thinking he was finished, he found he then had to go to a crossroad another click and a half away, which was the RV point, and be ready to move by 1800hrs.

Tricky all right, he thought. You're finished, but you're not finished. Footsore and fucked, he finally staggered into the RV at 1340hrs to find only one other person there – his mate Jack, who was heating up some water for his ration, which they were now allowed to eat.

Almost out on his feet, he asked Jack to heat him some water for his freeze-dry, which he had already taken out of his pack and dropped on the ground next to Jack's. "Sure, bro," said Jack. Pete lay wearily down, falling almost immediately into an exhausted sleep. When the cold eventually awoke him some hours later, the sun had almost set and it was getting dark very quickly. There were a dozen or more of the others at the RV by now, he saw as he wearily looked around. Most were sound asleep, although there were a couple of cookers going.

Jack was sitting there packed and ready to go. "I was just going to wake you," he said.

"Where's my ration?" Pete asked querulously.

"I tried to wake you when it was ready, bro, but you wouldn't wake up and I didn't want to waste it. So I ate it myself," said Jack with a mischievous smile on his face.

"Oh yeah?" asked Pete. "And how hard did you try and wake me?"

"This hard," said Jack and mouthed the word Pete silently. They both laughed and Pete said: "You fucking bastard." He didn't really mind, though. He'd had a better feed than a fucking freeze-dry. Some of the guys reckoned you could just about starve to death on those bastards because there was no goodness in them at all.

The pick-up never eventuated at 1800hrs and it was well after 2100hrs before any of the staff turned up. There were still only 27 candidates at the RV. Eleven had pulled the pin, it seemed, and one had gone missing after making only two checkpoints. The staff had to go and search for him. They found him all right. He'd fallen into a deep sleep while taking a break. They scratched him from the course immediately, and they weren't in a hell of a good a mood when they finally arrived. Consequently the 27 footsore aching and tired survivors found themselves doing a double hobble along the gravel roads for nearly an hour before they were finally allowed to cumbersomely board the still-moving truck.

Only one vehicle was needed now and they all somehow clumsily crowded on, back flap rolled down, and off they went under dire exhortation not to go to sleep, or else. Everyone was already absolutely fucked and it was only the end of day two. What were they going to have to do next?

It wasn't too far off midnight when the truck finally stopped, the back flap lifted and they were screamed at to de-bus. Climbing down somewhat stiffly and still half asleep (most of them had nodded off anyway) they discovered they were back at the SAS HQ. They were marched into a training shed, re-issued with one more freeze-dry and ordered to clean their weapons. They were all guilty of neglecting this over the past couple of days, something normally regarded as a cardinal sin.

While this was going on, a couple of troopers carried in a tea urn and several loaves of bread. The candidates hardly dared to hope for a cup of tea and some bread. That would be a feast, but it seemed too good to be true. But it was true. When the weapons were finished and inspected, the men were ordered to file through with their tin mug and received not tea, but even better – vegetable soup plus two slices of bread each. The staff stood around and reckoned they were spoiling them. So the food didn't last very long. Everyone bolted it just in case the staff changed their minds. But they didn't.

All too soon, it was back out on the road and doubling away again, although thankfully it was just back to the barracks. Here they were ordered to take another shower on another rather cold night with a frost probably on the way. No one passed on the wash this time and with a lot of whooping and laughter, they all took their turn in the freezing water.

Much to their surprise, they were then ordered to go to bed, which they all did with some alacrity. Wisely, most kept their clothes and boots on with their gear packed and ready to go. They were beginning to learn. Within 10 minutes there was not a conscious soul in the place. They only sound was exhausted snores.

They were so far gone that no one even heard the truck pull up outside the barracks at 0500hrs on a fine, frosty morning. The candidates had been asleep for only just over three hours. That was long enough, according to the staff, and if the lights and noise weren't enough to drag the candidates unwillingly out of their deep and exhausted repose, the staff weren't slow in assisting.

Most awoke reasonably quickly and were semi-switched-on straight away. But several had to be tipped on to the floor, none too gently either. All too soon, they all found themselves back on the truck, huddled together for warmth in the freezing cold and wondering where they were off to now.

They found that out just over an hour later when the truck stopped, the back flap was opened and they were ordered out. It was fucking cold and several of the guys who had draped their blankets around their shoulders were curtly ordered to put them away. "What'da ya think this is, a fucking school picnic?" one of the staff demanded. Well they were at a school of sorts by the look of it, but no one thought to make mention of that.

Pete knew where they were. He'd heard talk about this phase of the selection: Crossing the Meremere swamp. It was notorious for causing candidates to pull out and infamous after someone had died in the attempt on a previous course years ago.

They were in the grounds of a disused primary school backing on to the swamp, a victim of government cost-cutting, urban drift or both, which allowed the army to make use of the empty facilities. They were quickly organised into six groups of four and one of three, each issued with five-gallon plastic jerrycans full of water – three for the bigger groups and two for the smaller.

They'd be dropped off at various points around the huge swamp area, where the accompanying staff would give them their orders. As they completed their assigned task, the jerrycans would have to travel every step of the way with them, and remain full. Jesus, Pete thought, shaking his head. They were heavy bastards. And Jack wasn't in his group either. He wasn't really looking forward to this little lot. Apart from the one group which was starting from the old school, they were ordered back on to the truck. The jerrycans made it a tight squeeze but it wouldn't be too much longer before they entered the swamp.

Pete's group was dropped off along the gravel road adjoining the swamp and the staff member gave his orders. They had to be at a grid reference on the opposite side before 1800hrs. But because of supposed enemy activity, they could travel only through the swamp, not around it. It was pretty basic map reading: Find out where they were and where they had to go on the map, get the grid bearing, convert it to magnetic and off they go. It sounded simple and it was. With the aid of the staff member's torch, because it was still dark, they soon had it all sorted out. It was simple, all right – except for the swamp bit in between the two grid references.

The water was waist-high and fucking freezing and Pete felt his balls contract then disappear up to where ever it is they retreat to in just such a situation. One of their team, a short, five-foot-nothing Maori guy, found the water level was halfway up his chest, so they appointed him the bearing follower and track breaker, while the rest trailed behind carrying the jerrycans.

It was fucking hard yakka. The water level remained constant but there were plenty of weeds to be pushed through and flax bushes to be avoided, as well as the soft mud of varying depth to be ploughed through. The jerrycan carriers often found themselves waiting for their short track-breaker, whose task was turning out to be a real strength-sapping exercise. While waiting, they all put their jerrycans down and quickly noticed that they floated quite well at the top of the scummy water.

It didn't take too much more thought before the toggle ropes came off the webbing and the jerrycans were being towed, which was certainly a lot easier than carrying them, especially with the footing so unsteady. The track-breaker was getting noticeably slower and worn out, so eventually they all had to take turns at the front, which was by far the hardest job. At least no one could complain of blisters or chafe, though. They were all too fucking cold to feel anything in their lower halves. And it was no good stopping for a rest, either. If you sat down, the water would be over your head.

As the daylight grew and the sun weakly promised to come over the horizon, they ploughed steadily and mindlessly through the freezing, sucking, strength-sapping morass. But it was no good complaining, was it? After all, they'd all volunteered for this little holiday jaunt. Hadn't they?

The time slipped steadily away as they persevered. It was real thumb-up-bum stuff and later on, when Pete tried to recall that particular day, he found it very hard to remember much at all. Sometime in the late afternoon, the swamp became shallower – possibly because the winter hadn't been that wet yet. The going became knee deep, then only ankle deep. While this made for easier and faster walking, it meant they had to carry the jerrycans instead of dragging them. But it did make the track-breaker's job much easier for a while.

The water soon got deeper again, however, although never quite as deep as waist height. One of the guys began to flag badly as the dusk began to settle in, and kept saying he wanted to pull out. The others encouraged him, telling him they were almost there and he'd still have to walk out anyway, so he might as well stick with it. The accompanying staff member, who had trailed along at the back all day, said nothing. But he wasn't missing too much, either. They trundled on, considerably hampered now by the one who wanted to pull out. He became slower and slower, although to his credit he still towed his jerrycan. It was well after 1900hrs and long gone dark when they finally reached the far side and hauled themselves thankfully and wearily on to dry land.

The staff member ordered them to have a break and cook up their ration, then led their flagging companion away into the darkness. They didn't see him again.

It was freezing cold, looking rather like another frost was on the way, and it didn't take too long before they were shivering in their wet clothes. They made a joint decision to get into their dry ones and were sitting there with their blankets around their shoulders trying to keep warm when the staff member finally reappeared with the only two surviving members from another group, including Jack.

With a straight face he told them as they were staying for the night in that position and should make themselves as warm and comfortable as possible and be ready to move at 0500hrs the next day, then disappeared into the darkness. Comfortable? Sure. Warm? Sure. The man was an absolute comedian.

It was already cold enough and promising to get worse. They thought briefly about a fire but decided reluctantly against it. Then Jack had an idea: "We'll put one blanket down on the ground. Four of us lie on it on our sides, get as comfortable as we can, top and tailing. The fifth person then spreads the other four blankets on top of us and gets under at one end."

It wasn't much of a plan but it was about all they had. Pete ended up with the short straw and was last man in. It worked to a certain extent, with a couple of them managing to nod off briefly at various stages. But it was really too cold for any proper sleep.

It was almost a relief when, not long after midnight, two members of the staff turned up, saying the plan had changed. They now had to go back through the swamp to where they started from, immediately. You could almost hear the silence as the candidates lay stunned by this bit of intelligence.

"Come on! Come on! Up you get, you lot! Let's go! Now!" one of the staff shouted as they all slowly got to their feet.

When they had stowed their gear away and put on webbing and packs, they moved to the edge of the swamp where one of the staff asked: "Does anyone want to pull out? There's a cup of tea and a hot meal waiting back at the school. You can be warm, dry and have a belly full in just under an hour."

Silence.

"Come on, doesn't anyone want to pull out before you get all wet again?"

Silence.

"Well, don't everyone answer at once."

A voice said firmly: " No, we're all going back through, the whole lot of us." It was the shortest guy of all, the one who'd had the most trouble in the swamp.

"Don't say I didn't give you the chance, then. Let's go," said the disappointed-sounding staff member, and they slid back into the black freezing water and with their still dry clothes on. Yuck!

It was too dark to see where they'd pushed through on the way over, which might have made the going a bit easier. But on the bonus side, the staff appeared to have forgotten all about the jerrycans, which they'd piled off to one side the night before.

Half-expecting to be sent back for them at any moment, they ploughed back through the swamp, soon settling into a familiar rhythm, the moonlight glinting off the water and highlighting the gaps between the flax bushes for the track breaker.

Half an hour or so later they were all thoroughly wet, cold and anaesthetised from the waist down. Then: "Okay, new orders. Turn round. Back we go." Cunts.

By 0140hrs they were back on the dry again. "Okay, back to sleep. Ready to move on the road at 0500hrs." But there was not to be too much sleep for anyone that night. They dozed intermittently in their wet clothes then were woken by the cold, with everyone having to get up every once in a while and move around just to generate a bit of warmth.

Everyone was relieved when 0500hrs finally rolled around. They walked out to the road carrying the jerrycans which the waiting staff ordered them to leave stockpiled to one side while, surprise, surprise, they were doubled down to meet the truck. At least this warmed them up somewhat.

When all the groups had been picked up, the truck seemed a lot emptier. A quick count revealed only 19 survivors, a further eight having pulled out on the swamp phase. They weren't even half way through the course yet. Christ, at this rate there'd be no one left at the end.

They were back in camp just after 0700hrs, all still feeling a dreadful overdose of cold. They were sent for another cold shower and shave, and issued one clean set of clothes, supposedly to replace the wet and dirty set. But for most of them, both sets were now just as bad.

Taking a risk, they all decided to wash the dirty set in the shower with them and hang them out, putting on the clean ones. The risk was they may well end up going somewhere without having a chance to retrieve them. After the shower, it was down to the training shed to clean their filthy, mud-covered and in some cases rusty weapons. During this activity, the storeman arrived with a whole bunch of hotboxes and the tea urn.

The smell of hot food tantalized and teased them but, not wanting to get their hopes up, they kept their minds on the job at hand and pretended not to notice the food. There was stacks of it, too. Obviously enough had been ordered for the numbers there had been before they went into the swamp. But they had been sucked in before and waited, hoping against hope that they were going to get a decent feed at last.

The staff went through first and made a great show of walking past them their mess tins or plates full. Finally, the candidates were put out of their misery. "All right, line up you guys," said the comedian with the ever-present sly smile on his face. Nobody moved. "Aren't you hungry, then?" he asked. There was a sudden rush for the plates and the candidates filed through to get their food. Spaghetti, sausages, scrambled egg . . . the plates were heaped high. A couple of pieces of bread and a canteen of tea, even sugar if desired. The sugar got hammered.

They all retreated quickly back to their benches and for the next few minutes nothing could be heard but the ravenous 19 bolting their food, just in case it was another trick. But it wasn't, and they were even allowed seconds on the tea. Wonders would never cease. The squadron medic also put in an appearance and did the rounds, which granted them all a bit of a rest as it took some time for him to talk to them all.

Pete's feet were still dead, he was as skinny as a rake and suffering a bit of chafe. They all were pretty much in the same boat except the ones carrying blisters, who were really struggling. But nobody really wanted to admit to any injury at this stage. It may well have been regarded as a black mark or even worse, it might be recommended they be pulled out.

It was only a brief respite, however and all too soon they were ordered into the classroom for more testing, interviews and buddy ratings. When Pete looked around at who was left, he realised that of the 19, all the seven returnees from Singapore were still hanging in there.

After surviving some two hours in the classroom and really struggling to remain awake, they were doubled down to the concourse, although not, as they first thought, to go over it again. After some very quick instruction, they were chucked out of the rappelling tower, which was something entirely new for all of them.

When this activity was finished, it was over Red Hill with pack webbing and rifle. A 10-miler, run at a hectic pace. They all soon started feeling the pinch and it was no real surprise when three guys started struggling and gradually drifted off the back of the group.

This actually did the rest of them a favour as the staff slowed them down to see if the drifters could catch up. Eventually one did manage to tack on again during the downhill stretch, but the other two didn't and weren't sighted again. By the time they got back to camp it was after 1500hrs and there were now only 17 survivors.

It was straight into the swimming pool then, where they were bastardized around for an hour or so, although it seemed like much longer. The staff made sure they were all thoroughly saturated in the fucking freezing water before being doubled back to the barracks.

All were desperately tired by now, in need of a decent sleep and after changing into their by-now dry clothes and hanging out the wet ones, they were rather surprised to be ordered to bed. They didn't need any second invitations and the barracks quietened miraculously as the nearly exhausted survivors fell asleep immediately.

It was almost the same scenario as the previous morning. The truck arrived at 0400hrs but this time one of the boys was awake, heard it and hurriedly went round and roused the others so that when the staff did burst in, they were almost ready to go. Not that they had much to pack, but at least they had time to reclaim the still damp clothes off the line.

The usual story: On to the truck, flaps down and away, not so much yelling or abuse from the staff this time and the course were on the countdown. Day six, four more to rip. It wasn't as cold, either. There hadn't been a frost overnight and from the look of the clouds, it might rain. After about an hour and a half the truck stopped and they were ordered out.

They were outside the PTSU at Whenuapai Air Force Base. No surprises here – they'd finished the para course so a jump had probably always been on the cards. One of the para instructors eventually arrived and it was into the hangar for a spot of revision and briefing.

After the briefing came a pleasant surprise – a Land Rover arrived with hotboxes of air force food, always far better than the army issue. It was the best feed they'd had so far: Bacon, eggs, baked beans, sausages, bread and tea with plenty of sugar. They all made pigs out of themselves. Most ate until their shrunken stomachs felt uncomfortable, and several had to make a mad dash for the shithouse. As they waited for the plane to be made ready, many of them took the opportunity to readjust their webbing and packs, which by now hung loosely on their gaunt, food- starved frames.

Pete generally had a small roll of fat round his belly that quickly disappeared when he went into the field for any length of time but soon came back after a couple of days of fresh rations and booze. But this had long since disappeared. They were all skinny as rakes, and the fact that they had to use only the issued webbing on the course with its metal clips, and not the much more comfortable stuff of their own devise, had invariably caused chaffing.

Two hours later they jumped in two sticks, up north somewhere near Warkworth and the Maharangi pine forests, according to the map they'd been issued just before boarding the plane. The game was really on in earnest now. It was a map-reading circuit and they'd been warned the trackers would be out in force. No mercy could be expected if they were caught.

The landing zone was a large empty paddock in which they landed well spread out and there was plenty of shit around to testify to the previous recent inhabitants. Pete was in the second stick. Just before he landed, he saw one of the staff heading his way and thought for one awful moment he been caught already. But no, there was a reasonable breeze blowing and one of the guys had completely misjudged it and injured himself on landing. He was out of it, leaving only 16. Pete hurriedly packed up his chute, carried it to the gate as ordered and, leaving it with the others, headed straight up hill to the bush line. The quicker he was out of sight, the better. He was soon joined by several of the others with exactly the same idea, although they all probably had different grid references to head for.

They just wanted to get out of the open first before sorting out the best route to take. Pete didn't like the situation much, the four of them all together and heading in the same direction. They stood out like dog's balls, sitting ducks for the trackers if they were around.

As they headed up a rough bulldozed track through some scrub and gorse, he stopped suddenly and ducked off into a large stand of gorse, thinking to let the others get ahead before he carried on. The other three carried on, and had just got to the top of the hill and nearly disappeared over the skyline when Pete heard all this whooping and yelling. Peering out of his cover, he saw that the three had been sprung by a four-man tracking team.

They were giving them arseholes, making them do press-ups and sit-ups, crawl along on their stomachs through the cow shit, emptied their packs, confiscated their ration, threw their blankets in the shit. The bastardization went on for 10 minutes or more and Pete huddled even deeper into his gorse bush, hoping the tracking team didn't come further down the hill or they'd see him for sure. After a while, when it went quiet, he looked up slowly while trying not to move at the same time and saw the three victims slowly repacking their belongings then eventually moving off out of sight.

He remained in that bush, almost oblivious to the sharp gorse spikes, for at least another 20 minutes before cautiously emerging and crawling on his hands and knees through the scrub to the top of the hill and carefully looking around. The trackers and their victims were out of sight and the forest was only about 500 or 600 metres away. He lay completely still for a further 10 minutes and, seeing no movement, decided it was no good just lying there and it was time to take a risk and make a dash for the trees. Three fences and what seemed like a lifetime later, but in truth was probably not even 10 minutes, he breathlessly gained the forest and plunged deep into the welcoming cover, where he sat down and began his calculations.

Another hour found him well on his way to the first checkpoint, on a bearing, padding almost silently through the soft curtain of pine needles beneath the trees – the safest way, he'd thought – and using extreme care in crossing the forest roads. Again, the map-reading was easy. It was what might be between the checkpoints that was the problem and was to be avoided at all costs.

The weather was starting to turn a bit shitty. A strong wind was blowing and it looked like it might rain. That wouldn't help them at all either, with no wet-weather gear. He settled into the by now very familiar distance-covering gait and pushed on. Only four days to go. Only four days to go.

The wind got up quite badly that night, which probably kept the rain away. But it made it bloody hard to hear anything. This would work both ways, though. Pete had cleared two checkpoints during the day without seeing anything of the trackers or even any other candidates. The grid reference for his third checkpoint was out in open farmland, however, and meant he'd have to leave the cover of the trees, which he wasn't so keen on. At 1643hrs, when he reached the edge of the forest and saw just how open the farmland was, he decided he'd better wait until dark before carrying on. Pulling back into the trees, he settled down to wait and soon, despite his best intentions, he nodded off.

Waking with a sudden start, he checked his watch and found it was just before 2300hrs. Fuck! He'd slept for nearly six hours. It was still very windy, with a touch of driven rain about, as he set off again. He wasn't feeling too bad after his unplanned sleep. The bottoms of his feet, the old parched leather, were still asleep, and he hoped they'd stay there. Apart from a swollen ankle, courtesy of the jump, and an old rugby breakage that bothered him occasionally, he wasn't in too bad a shape. Nothing a decent feed wouldn't fix, anyway.

Two hours later, he entered his third checkpoint, finding it quite easily because they had a lantern going. He got the grid reference for his next one and was soon on his way again. There had been two more pull-outs in the small camp. Again, he'd not been allowed to talk to them. But it was obvious the rigors of the past six days were really starting to take their toll. What did that make, 14 left out of, what, 56? Pete shook his head and wondered how many of the Singapore boys were still left.

Because it was now nearly 0200hrs he decided to take a risk, hoping the trackers would be in bed by now, and use the ridgelines for ease of travel and navigation purposes, plus less chance of accident. He was travelling easily and making good time too in the blustery near-raining conditions, when he nearly shit himself.

Walking along a bit of a ridgeline that seemed to be taking him in the right direction, he suddenly heard a voice calling and looking to his right saw three dim figures lying in among the ti-tree. Thinking he'd bumped into the trackers' camp, he was just about to bolt, when he heard his name called and a figure rise and limp toward him. It was Dave, one of his Singapore mates. They had a yarn for a couple of minutes, with Dave suggesting that perhaps he stay there till the morning, then move on with them. But Pete had already had his sleep and said he'd push on, a fortuitous decision that saved his arse from being caught by the trackers – as the other three were later that morning.

He rocked up to the next checkpoint at 0545hrs, having to wake the staff member to get his next grid reference. Rather surprisingly, because the staff usually weren't very talkative, he was informed that there had been five more pull-outs so far on this phase, leaving only 11 of them still persevering. The toll was mounting. Quickly doing his map reading calculations by the light of the staff member's torch, he set off into the darkness for the penultimate checkpoint, but stopped after going less than 10 metres to take off and readjust his pack because it was chaffing him again.

The staff member must have thought he'd long departed so Pete overheard him on the radio talking to base: "Candidate 7 has just left my loc bound for checkpoint 5. Inform the tracking groups. They'll probably pick him up in the valley if they're quick.

"I'll inform you when candidate 13 departs here also, he's the other one the trackers haven't picked up yet, over"

Pete smiled as he moved quietly away so as not to alert the staff member that he'd overheard. Candidate 13 was Jack and he was 7, and he was not going to go anywhere near that bloody valley if he could help it. The bastards were really trying to stack him up. Well, he had other ideas. He continued on until it began to get light, when he stopped under the cover of a grove of trees. The wind had backed off some by now but that had only allowed the clouds to settle in more ominously. It began to rain lightly.

He studied the map. He could reach the next checkpoint from the opposite side rather than using the valley, something he hoped they wouldn't expect. He would have to walk almost 2km further. But even allowing for the six hours he lost sleeping, he felt he was still all right for time, especially when compared with some of the others who were obviously struggling both physically and mentally. He set off in almost in a detached frame of mind, well down on energy and condition but determined not to let the course or the staff beat him. As the morning wore on and the wind abated, it began to piss down.

His calculation of 2km of extra walking proved just a trifle optimistic. The original plan would have forced him to traverse several ridgelines, putting him in plain view for miles around. So he had to contour and cross-grain in an endeavour to remain unseen. Consequently, it was early afternoon before he made his final approach, using every bit of cover and dead ground he could and surprising the hell out of the TF captain manning the checkpoint, who'd been mostly staring in the opposite direction, no doubt expecting him to come that way.

"Oh, there you are," he said, "I 've been looking out for you. You should have been here hours ago, you know?" he accused Pete. "I . . . I had a bit of a break sir," Pete said, not wanting to let on he knew he was being set up.

"Well, you'd better get on with it then," said the captain, giving him the next and final grid reference. The captain was suspiciously and unusually helpful, even going as far as pointing out the best way to go to get to the RV, a disused cow shed some five clicks away.

Pete thanked him and shambled off in the direction indicated until out of sight of the checkpoint, then quickly headed off eastwards. He found himself some reasonable cover from prying eyes and from the by-now persistent rain, and worked out his next move. He had plenty of time, with six hours to go before they had to be at the RV. But he knew if he went the way the captain had indicated, he was more than likely going to get caught. He saw there was a gravel access road a couple of valleys over, which meandered around a bit but eventually ended up less than a click from the cowshed. He decided to take a risk on using that.

It continued raining heavily as he started off again, stiffly at first as his body protested at the constant use but gradually warming to its task. The only good thing about the rain being that it would make visibility very poor. He hadn't been on the gravel road and striding it out determinedly for more than five minutes when a vehicle sluiced suddenly up behind him unheard and stopped before he could get into cover. If it had have been any of the staff, he'd have been fucked. But fortunately it was only the rural delivery man who, with great country-style hospitality, offered him a lift, soaked and all as he was. Pete dropped his pack and accepted in a flash. Anything was better than the rain and walking on that gravel road.

He sat as far back in the seat as he could after the driver had cleared it of the parcels and mail that had been on it. The delivery man laughed.

"Don't want to be seen, eh, all you mad eggs doing that SAS thing? Old Joe up the road told me. Don't worry, I won't say a word. It's pretty hard yakka, I heard. You hungry?"

Pete nodded enthusiastically and the driver handed him a plastic lunchbox. "Get into that," he said. "Finish it off." Needing no second invitation Pete opened the box, finding four sandwiches and a big lump of fruitcake. It was a feast! He quickly crammed a sandwich into his mouth.

"Where are ya going?" the driver asked. Between mouthfuls, Pete told him. "Yeah, I know the place," the driver said. "I'll drop ya off in some trees right near there. It'll only take ya few minutes then and you'll be outa the rain."

Pete normally didn't even like fruitcake, but with all his energy about used up and his body craving fuel, it tasted absolutely delicious. All too soon they reached the place the driver had mentioned and it was time for Pete get out. But while he was still cold, wet and miserable, the food had injected much-needed energy back into his system. If he could reach the cowshed undiscovered, he should have some time up his sleeve for a rest, too. Thanking the driver profusely, he moved quickly off the road into the dismal, damp and rapidly darkening afternoon. He'd had a bit of luck there and didn't really want to tempt fate too much further.

Jack had been holed up in a bit of scrub half way down the front side of the ridgeline running parallel to the one the penultimate checkpoint was on, and had a uphill good view of it. He too had walked all night, found this position early on in the morning and knowing he wasn't too far away from the checkpoint, had stopped for a rest and gone to sleep as well. The cold and rain had woken him several times and he'd seen Pete go in, so had waited for a while before going in himself, not wanting to give the impression that they'd been travelling together. He had been accused of this earlier on in the course when he had holed up near a checkpoint to make sure the way in was clear first, seen another candidate get in unmolested, so had followed him.

The staff didn't really understand, especially the pakeha ones. He had been bought up in the backblocks of the rugged Ureweras by his grandparents, and had been going pig-hunting on his own from when he was about 10. He knew a lot of the old Maori bush lore and only his mate Pete had any sort of an idea how much at home he was in the bush. And it just wasn't Jack's way to boast about anything. As far as he was concerned, the trackers weren't going to catch him. No way.

After a quarter hour or so of watching, he was just going to stand up and move on, when he heard a slight noise from behind and stayed completely still scarcely daring to breathe. A three-man tracking team doubled down the hill and passed his position only about 15 metres away. He worried momentarily about them finding his tracks then quickly realised they were moving much too fast to be tracking. They hurried on down the hill, then up to the checkpoint where the captain, waving his arms about vigorously, was obviously indicating which way Pete had gone.

Jack had had his suspicions about them being stacked up after having had a couple of close calls not long after leaving other checkpoints himself. Now it was confirmed. He waited until the tracking team was well out of sight before rising and making a quick move toward the comparative safety of the checkpoint, thinking that hopefully he'd get in and out while they were still chasing Pete. After that, well, he'd just have to take his chances.

It had just gone 1600hrs, still pissing down and growing really gloomy, when Pete made the comparative shelter of the cowshed, surprisingly finding it empty. He'd at least expected to find Jack there. Apart from the odd leak here and there, the old, once-painted-red rusty iron roof provided good shelter from the weather and, best of all, it was half full of bales of hay, at least something soft to rest on. He had about four hours' grace, according to what the captain had told him. But you could take that with a grain of salt, too. The staff would change things quickly if it suited them, and what was it they kept saying? Flexibility is the keynote.

Still, he should have at least a couple of hours up his sleeve anyway, and if any more of the candidates went missing, well, who knows? He cleared a spot on the crumbling and cracked concrete floor, opened his cooker, lit a piece of hexamine, dropped it into the cooker and placed a mug of water on top.

He was still ravenous, even after eating what the rural delivery man had given him. Even the freeze-dry had some sort of an attraction. Stripping completely, he used the spare pants from his pack and dried his body thoroughly. He stood and looked down at himself, the first real chance he'd really had to in more than a week. Christ, he'd lost some weight. His stomach had completely disappeared, his hip bones seemed to protrude right out like great fucking handle bars, and his legs, hands and arms were covered in minor scratches and bruises.

There were chafe marks where his webbing and pack had been rubbing against his rapidly dissolving torso, and the bottoms of his feet were still completely numb. The skin of his soles was a lot thicker than normal, too, with a couple of healthy corns developing. Add a bit of toe jam and the swollen ankle as well, plus the inclement weather, lack of food and sleep and near total exhaustion...he was in great shape, all right, he thought wryly, but he did volunteer and he'd been warned he'd be sorry.

Suddenly feeling the cold, he hurriedly put his dry clothes on, draped the blanket round his shoulders and reluctantly deciding it was better to be ready to move, donned his wet socks and boots again. By this time the water was not too far off the boil and he turned his attention to the freeze-dry. The meal took only a few minutes to demolish, by which time it was fully dark and he was just thinking about maybe having a gonk. Then a twang and vibration of wire close by startled him into alertness.

He hurriedly put on his webbing and, grabbing his rifle, moved into the darkest part of the old shed and took cover. He was supposed to be safe while in the RV but as they'd all found to their cost, some of the staff had their own agenda at times. Shortly three figures filed silently into the shed, a torch went on, traversed the interior and stopped at the pack, which he'd forgotten in the rush. A voice called: "Anyone here?"

Seeing he was lumbered anyway, Pete answered: "Yeah, me." He stood with his rifle in the aim and pointing at the three.

There was a bit of a lull in the darkness, then when the torch finally focused on him, the holder said: "It's you, Barron. Well done. You can relax, you're in a safe area now. But be ready to move by 2000." With that, the three turned and filed out into the bad weather again, obviously having more fish to fry.

Pete smiled. He knew they'd been all out after him and they couldn't understand why they hadn't at least seen him. Well, it was too late now. He settled down for some much-needed rest and despite his best intentions he was sound asleep within a few minutes. Jack came in stealthily, wet, cold and miserable but undetected some two-and-a-half-hours later and found four other people already in the RV. Three of them, including Pete, were sound asleep.

He'd sat off for a while, knowing the trackers were out there somewhere. Sure enough, he'd eventually seen some blurred figures break cover from some trees near the farm race the candidates would probably use if they came directly from the previous checkpoint. They'd actually caught two of the others there and fucked them round something chronic before letting them go. But they'd really been after Jack and Pete, the only ones they hadn't caught yet. They'd obviously got sick of waiting and moved out, betraying their presence to the ever-watchful Jack

Just to be sure, he'd circled right around and come in from the other side, which offered the most cover and dead ground. He would have been extremely hard to pick up in the dark. Jack, too, had lost a lot of weight, but the miserable conditions didn't seem to affect him quite as much as the others. He stayed in his wet gear as he heated up the water for the freeze-dry.

By 2000hrs there were still no staff and only eight candidates at the RV. Jack woke Pete and the others up and they all reluctantly readied for the next phase. Another candidate straggled in some 20 minutes later and two of the staff finally turned up with another in tow just before 2100hrs.

One more sensible person had pulled out, they were informed as they lined up in single file out in the race. Did anyone else want to follow suit? But no one even replied and they were doubled stiffly away toward the road. Each of the survivors was now having to dig deep. Not only were they well down on energy, condition and sleep, but most were carrying some sort of minor injury as well. Only two days to go, only two days to go.

The truck met them on the gravel road Pete had travelled up earlier and it was another mobile embus, very awkward as tired and wet as they were, with great potential for an accident. Jack showed as the tower of strength he was. He reached the truck first, scrambled on to the tray, dropped his pack and rifle, then man-handled the rest of them on, grabbing them by the webbing. He almost had to physically lift a couple of them who just couldn't find the energy to swing themselves up. If it hadn't been for his efforts, neither would have made it.

Unfortunately the truck ride was all too short and it was only half an hour or so before it stopped, the flap lifted and they were curtly ordered to debus again. As they crawled out into the raining and windy night, they could hear the sound of waves on a nearby shore. Looking around, they saw they were at a jetty on a riverbank near the middle of a town. It was the Warkworth town jetty and tied up alongside were two Zodiacs, each manned by a couple members of the staff. They were quickly split up, five to each Zodiac. Pete found himself on the one being piloted by the comedian and an offsider.

They set off down the river, which had quite a swell running, heading for the mouth from where they could still hear waves breaking heavily on the shore, even above the noise of the outboards. It was obviously a rough old night out there.

One of the Zodiacs was equipped with a radio and as they approached the river mouth the crew were called up and told that the activity was going to be cancelled as it was far too rough. They were to head back. As the Zodiacs turned and headed back, the candidates found themselves having to sing songs or tell jokes. If the staff didn't like their efforts, they had to jump over the side, minus rifle but with the rest of their gear on. Of course, everyone ended up over the side at some stage, hanging on for grim death to the ropes running along the gunnel and being towed along by the Zodiac.

This went on for what seemed like hours while the wind and rain raged, but eventually they found themselves back at the jetty. If the candidates and their gear hadn't been thoroughly saturated before, they were now. It was well on towards midnight when they doubled out of Warkworth again, in single file, now with nearly as many staff as there were candidates to harry and harass them. It seemed to take forever as they were shunted through various Warkworth suburbs then out the back way and uphill towards State Highway 1.

Everyone had already reached deep within themselves for strength and determination, and for most there wasn't a hell of a lot left as they all struggled to maintain the pace. Pete found his swollen ankle now suddenly very painful, having given it a bit of a knock in the river, and he drifted to the back of the group as they ran up hill. Several of the staff began harassing him as he hung on desperately to the rear. Thankfully, the back of the truck suddenly loomed out of the darkness when they reached the crest, then began moving slowly away from them. Jack did his thing again and when Pete made a desperate lunge for the back, he found himself physically lifted upwards and deposited unceremoniously on the tray. "Thanks bro," gasped Pete, sprawled on the floor with almost all of the others in a similar state.

"We've come too far to leave you behind now, boy. Hang in there, we're nearly home," said Jack, alone in still standing.

The truck stopped momentarily while the flap was lowered and they set off again. Where were they going this time and what was going to happen next?

Most of them were nearly at the end of their tether. They'd never been so wet, cold starving or miserable at time in their lives. And with the generator not charging any more, the will was fading rapidly. If they'd had to get out and run again that night, it's very probable that most of them would have pulled out on the spot. But whether the staff realised this or not, they'd never know. The truck ride lasted till the early hours of the following morning. When it finally stopped and they were ordered to debus sometime after 0500hrs, they found themselves at a country airfield. They eventually discovered they were on the outskirts of Kaitaia.

They were issued one more ration and when told they could either eat it straight away or keep it for later, most opted for the former. Mercifully for the survivors, who'd had a miserable cold night in their wet clothes on the truck, dozing off occasionally before being woken by the cold, it wasn't raining. As the day slowly dawned, it even held a promise of sunshine.

As they waited resignedly for the next phase to begin, they were ordered to begin cleaning their weapons. Contrary to the normal order of things, nearly all of them were in a shocking state by now. They candidates had all been that busy just trying to keep up with the pace, they'd not found the time to do much else.

An hour later, much to their surprise, the weapons were collected by the staff. As they all wondering what was afoot, the mystery deepened when an air force Iroquois helicopter arrived. Once the chopper had shut down, they were finally put out of their misery with a briefing about the next phase. The chopper would drop them off singly at points all over the north and they had to be back in camp at Papakura by 1600hrs the next day or face removal from the course. There was little time to talk about any of this because as soon as the chopper had warmed up again, they were ordered on board and it soon disappeared over the horizon.

Pete was dropped off on a beach, a large pine plantation in the background, somewhere on the east coast, although just exactly where he didn't know. As soon as the chopper departed, he walked wearily along the beach, searching for a road inland, and picked up a branch to use as a stave. Before too long he located the track he was looking for and headed inland at as good a pace as his body would allow. He hit the tar seal in just under two hours and turned south, on the road again.

Two cars passed by in the next half hour without stopping, even though he had his thumb out. Mind you, he couldn't really blame them. He looked as rough as guts, gaunt, unshaven, in black filthy clothes. He probably wouldn't have stopped either. The third car did, however, and it was no wonder. It was a very curious policeman, driving an ordinary car.

"Mind telling me who you are and what you're doing here, mate?" he asked.

Pete hesitated, then decided he might as well tell the truth. "I'm on the SAS selection course. I have to be back in camp by tomorrow afternoon."

The cop laughed. "One of those mad bastards, are you? I can give you a lift through to Kaeo if it'll help, mate. I'm stopping there, though."

Pete jumped at the chance, now knowing roughly where he was. "That'll be beaut," he said, "more chance of picking up another lift from there, too."

He jumped in and after a couple of kilometres and a bit of chat he was fast asleep, much to the cop's amusement.

He was shaken awake in Kaeo and the policeman flicked him $5. "Here, get yourself a feed at the takeaway before you go, mate. Good tucker there."

"Thanks mate, that's bloody good of you, I'll buy you a beer sometime, if I can," Pete volunteered.

"You just pass the course, mate. You look as though you deserve to. You're all skin and bone," the policeman said and disappeared into the station.

Ten minutes later, after scoffing a pie and with a couple of sandwiches in a bag, Pete hobbled south, happier now knowing where he was and that he had a plan. He had spent a couple of seasons at Moerewa freezing works and had played rugby locally. As far as he knew, a couple of old teammates were still living at home with their parents in Opua. Their father had been in the Maori Battalion and had been particularly pleased when Pete had taken the time to visit before heading overseas the first time.

He decided to head there, knowing they'd help him – perhaps lending him a bus fare or something. He didn't really want to hitch all the way back to Pap. His leg was giving him arseholes. A car suddenly stopped and he walked up to the window. A woman in her 30s said: "I don't usually pick up hitchhikers but I was talking to the policeman at Kaeo and he told me to watch out for you. I'm a commercial traveller, I've got business in Kerikeri but then I'm going through to Paihia. I should be there around three, is that any good to you?"

Pete, silently thanking the policeman, took the proffered ride. Anything was better than walking now. The leg bothered him continually.

His mates' father, Ray, laughed like hell when he finally hobbled in not long after 1700. "Eh, boy," he said, "what the hell are you doing? You've lost all your hinu."

Pete dropped his pack, flopped down heavily in the seat that had always been by the front door, and began to explain. Ten minutes or so later, it was almost as though he was in heaven – half asleep, soaking in a hot bath, and he could smell the big feed Ray was cooking up for him. Fresh fried fish. He was drooling.

He'd run right into luck here. Ray, a self-employed painter, didn't have a lot on at the moment and wouldn't hear of him catching the bus to Auckland. He insisted he'd run him all the way back to Pap himself, first thing in the morning. Be there by mid-morning at the latest, he reckoned.

For the first time in nine days, Pete relaxed, feeling everything was under control at last. After a couple of beers and a big feed that he found he couldn't finish because his stomach had shrunk, Pete collapsed into bed and slept solidly for 10 hours, only waking when Ray shook him solidly at 0600hrs.

"Come on, boy," he said. "You've got some travelling to do yet. You missed Ken. He got home about 10 last night and had to leave early this morning. He said to say good day, ya honky bastard."

Pete smiled as he put on his black clothes that had been washed and tumble-dried the previous night. Ray had done that. His missus was away visiting a relation.

After a bit of breakfast – some of the cold fish left from the previous night – they were on their way. Pete relaxed in the front seat, dozing off occasionally but thoroughly enjoying every minute of the ride. When Ray dropped him near a grove of trees at the back of the camp, it wasn't much after 1000hrs. "Thanks, Ray," he said. "I owe you one. I'll catch up with you."

"No worries there, boy," was the reply. "You just pass the course, then come up and visit us and we'll talk about it then. Maybe a trip to the pub, eh? Ka kite." With a big smile, Ray drove away.

Pete ducked into the trees and decided to stay there until at least lunchtime. The weather was fine and it was far too early to be going in. He certainly didn't want to be doubling anywhere, so he made himself comfortable and settled down to wait.

Hobbling in the side gate at 1345hrs, he ducked around behind the barracks, using them as cover to get as close as he could to the SAS compound before having to break into a trot. He ran into a WRAC he knew. "Pete!" she said, looking shocked. "What happened to you? You've lost your arse." She burst out laughing.

"I'll see you in the bar," he replied and kept moving. He hauled up outside the training wing under the critical eye of a couple of SAS troopers, halted himself thankfully, stood at ease and waited. A few minutes later, the sergeant major appeared. He snapped to attention while he was being looked over.

"At ease, Barron," he was told. "The testing phase of the course is now over, and interviews will commence after 1600hrs, when hopefully the rest of the candidates are back. Go back to the barracks and get yourself cleaned up, then start on your gear. If you've got any medical problems, the squadron medic will be there around 1500. Talk to him then. That's about all I've got for you now. Any questions?"

"No, sergeant major."

"Away you go then. Oh, and Barron, congratulations on finishing this phase. You've had some shithouse weather to contend with and you've done well to get this far. Apart from that, you'll have to wait for your interview to find out any more."

"Thank you, sergeant major," Pete said, turning and hobbling away with a sigh of relief. Thank Christ for that, he thought, I'd have been hard pushed to raise another gallop.

On reaching the barracks, he found the shower was running warm again and in it was none other than his old mate Jack, who'd got in half an hour previously. Despite the aches and pains, they were soon enthusiastically swapping stories.

The candidates waited, nervously, silently and expectantly in the classroom. They were being called in one by one and interviewed by a panel consisting of the major, a captain, the sergeant major and the civvy shrink.

"What the fuck's that bitch doing in there," Pete had snorted. He didn't like her and anyway, she'd said he wouldn't pass. Well here he was, just.

But it wasn't all over. Ten of them had finished but of the three who'd had been interviewed so far, one had been told he wasn't being accepted. He been told to get a bit more experience then come back and do it all again

He'd come out extremely downhearted. "All that for nothing," was all he'd say before lapsing into a morose silence.

Pete felt a momentary loss of confidence. He didn't much like the fact she was having so much say in matters. What would she know, anyway? He waited uneasily for his turn to be interviewed.

"Physically and mentally we think you've done really well on this course Lance-Corporal Barron," the major was saying, "and could handle anything the squadron threw at you in the future." Pete felt a wave of elation pass through him.

"However," the major continued, "the psych's report suggests that you are the sort of person who after we spend the time and money training you up to an acceptable standard, would be just as likely to tell us to stick it up our arse. What do you say to that?"

Pete fairly bristled and glared at the psych. He began thinking desperately. "Well sir, if you remember, the psych also said that I wouldn't get this far. Well, all I can say is sir, here I am."

"Good answer, Barron," cut in the sergeant major and turned to the major. "For my money, sir, I'd give him the chance. I had a report about him from Captain Murray and apart from the odd stuff-up on the booze, which he sorted out, he apparently did really well over there. So my vote's yes."

"What about you, captain?" the major asked the officer sitting next to him, who happened to be the captain who'd manned the final checkpoint up near Warkworth.

The captain cleared his throat, obviously giving himself time to think. "Well sir," he said, "I was really impressed with the two we couldn't catch. They both displayed good map- reading and evasion skills. That's just the sort of person we need in the squadron, so my vote's yes for both of them."

The major turned expectantly to the psych, who just rolled her eyes and gave an almost imperceptible nod. The major said: "Lance Corporal Barron, we are prepared to offer you the opportunity to remain with the squadron for cycle training. Just remember, until you complete this and become a fully badged member of the unit, you remain attached to the battalion and can be returned there at any time. The training is long and arduous and a small percentage do fail. So work hard, keep your nose clean, and hopefully we'll see you still here in six months' time wearing a different colour beret. Congratulations. That's all. Dismissed."

Pete snapped to attention and floated out the door, sore leg completely forgotten. He'd bloody made it and he reckoned nothing they could throw at him could ever be as hard as what he'd just been through. He was in and so was Jack, by the look of it. And that was all that mattered. They'd both made it! You bloody beauty!

WHO CALLED THE COOK A BASTARD?

The food in the Thousand Man Mess at Waiouru was absolute shite, so the five squadron boys on the instructors' course had soon taken to cooking up at night in one of their rooms on the second floor of the barracks.

Totally against camp standing orders, of course, but the boys were going to be there for five weeks and couldn't stomach what was being dished out – more especially at dinner time, when it seemed to be at its worst. It was all right if you were in the first 100 diners or so, but after that the quality deteriorated rapidly to the stage where you could hardly recognise what it had originally started life as. To be fair to the cooks, it was probably near impossible to maintain a decent standard with two Basics, all the various courses to feed and the mess operating to near capacity the whole time.

Everyone knew that when you went to Waiouru and "dined in" at the ORs' mess, it was usually fatty meat and bubble and squeak. The boys soon decided to take the law into their own hands. They all pitched in with the money and someone would shoot into Waiouru, buy pork bones, bacon bones or brisket, and some potatoes, kumara and cabbage. Then they'd all gather in one room, lock the door to keep out unwanted guests, and have a big boil-up using the gas cooker and bottle brought down from Pap precisely for this reason.

Occasionally they'd also have a few beers while waiting for the food to cook, which would have been regarded as an even more heinous breach of standing orders if they were caught. They hadn't been as yet, so they continued on with the practice, although on this particular night there was no beer. Too much work and rehearsal still to do.

On leaving the unit in Papakura they'd been warned of the dire consequences if they fucked up. "The training unit staff love nothing better than to get dirt on squadron guys. We don't want any RTUs, so keep your noses clean," they'd been sternly warned. But it seemed the warning had fallen on deaf ears.

"What a cunt of a day. I'll be glad when this fucken' course is over. Too much brain work for me." The speaker was Paul Munday, known to one and all as Kutu because he once got caught scratching his arse on parade and the drill sergeant asked him if he had kutus.

He was a happy-go-lucky, cheeky fella and very outspoken, which didn't go down too well in some quarters, especially among some officers. But the bookwork, along with all the preparation and study required on this course, wasn't really his forte and he struggled a bit at times. His mates were adamant he wasn't going to "blow his arse" and were dragging him by his bootlaces stage by stage through the course, successfully thus far.

"Come on, Kutu," teased Rob, "you're loving it. Staying up till two in the morning doing lesson plans, plus all the little tests in the mornings, out on the parade ground in the frost. It's your scene, man. It wouldn't surprise me if they wanted you to stay on as an instructor."

"Fuck off, ya cheeky cunt," said Kutu, laughing. "They'll never get me down here. It's the bloody arsehole of New Zealand. I'd get out first."

The others all laughed. There were five of them in the room and none was enjoying the unaccustomed classroom time. But they all needed to complete the course to become instructors, and of course for promotion as well. The general sentiment was: "Well, we have to do this, so let's do it, pass the first time and not have to come back again." So they all helped each other with the writing and rehearsing of their lesson plans, though sometimes they found themselves still up in the wee small hours trying to put the finishing touches on some of the more troublesome assignments.

They were slowly getting there, with over half the course gone. Only about three and a half weeks to go. They were all eagerly looking forward to completion.

A loud knock at the door suddenly silenced the conversation and they all looked at each other for a few seconds before Kutu took it upon himself to respond. "Fuck off!" he yelled.

This prompted an outraged bellow: "This is the orderly officer! Open this door! Immediately!" The boys looked helplessly at each other. "Fuck," said Frankie. "We're gone."

Rob opened the door and the orderly sergeant swept into the room, closely followed by a highly irate second lieutenant. "Room! Room shun!" The sergeant called them up to attention while the officer's attention focused totally on the bubbling pot.

"Cooking in the barracks, eh! That's expressly forbidden in standing orders!" And then off he went, rattling on about standing orders for what seemed like five minutes but was probably only two. Finally came what they expected: "You're all on charge! You guys should know better. You're not in Papakura now, you know. You can't get away with this sort of behaviour here. This is a training establishment with standards to be maintained and examples to be set. Sergeant?"

"Sah!"

"Take their names!"

The orderly sergeant quickly whipped out his notebook and began doing the rounds.

"And anyway," the officer continued as the names were being taken. "What's wrong with the food at the mess?" The boys all looked helplessly at each other and remained mute.

"Well?" the officer asked again after a few seconds. "What's wrong with the food at the mess?"

After more hesitation, Kutu finally spoke out. He was never one to keep his mouth closed for very long. "Sir," he said. "I wouldn't feed that shit to my dog."

The officer was totally gob-smacked at this answer and his mouth worked silently, opening and closing a few times before the words finally came. "Well," he asked. "Have you done anything about it?"

Again, no immediate reply.

"Have you done anything about it? There are channels to lay a complaint, you know"

"Yes sir," it was old Kutu again. "We've complained, sir. Twice."

"And what happened?" snapped the impatient officer.

"Well, what happened?"

"It got worse, sir," said a highly indignant Kutu.

The officer cracked up. He lost it completely, laughing helplessly along with the boys, and even the very regimental and upright sergeant had a bit of a guffaw. It took some seconds for the officer to recover himself.

"Look, you guys," he finally managed to say. "I know the food here isn't that flash. But that doesn't mean you can cook in the barracks. I'll let you go with a warning this time, but don't let me catch you at it again or I'll throw the book at you. Understand?"

The boys all nodded.

"Go down to one of the training huts, go out in the field, or the rugby grounds, or something. But do not, I say again, do not; let me catch you cooking in my barracks again."

He stopped and looked sternly at each soldier in turn. "Do you fully understand?"

"Yes sir," Kutu again.

"Sergeant!" the officer said.

"Room! Room shun!" The pair swept out of the room.

The boys waited for a long time before they all whooped with relief. "On ya, Kutu. Ya certainly got us out of the shit there," said Rob as Kutu's back was being pounded all round.

"You all owe me a beer," he said, "I know how to handle the hierarchy, boy. All ya gotta do is bamboozle them with brains."

Rob replied: "Well, let's see you do it to the instructors on the course, then." This prompted loud, whooping laughter.

TWO-AND-A-HALF FINGERS LEFT

Wednesday, sports day, and the big game on in earnest. The annual rugby challenge between the Gunners and the Squadron. No quarter expected and none given.

There had been a bit of bloodshed in the past. Nothing too serious, just the odd punch-up now and again. All in good fun, and they would be mates again back in the rugby club afterwards. This time they had brought in an outside ref because last year there had been murmurs of favouritism.

Even though the Squadron had won for three years running, the Gunners were the favourites this year because the Squadron had three troops away on deployment, preventing at least half a dozen top players from taking part. But it was no use crying over spilt milk. They would just have to make do with what they had.

The Gunners knew they were in with a shot this year because of the depleted Squadron and apparently some big bets had been offered and accepted in the sergeants' mess over the past few days.

At the Squadron team meeting after training the previous evening, the coach, Sergeant Bob Michaels, and the manager, Staff Heta, had laid out the plan, such as it was. It was very simple.

Some of the team members this year weren't even regular rugby players, but the one advantage they did have was that they were all very fit. The tactic of the day was to run the Gunners hard until their big forwards began to feel the pinch, which would hopefully slow them down and blunt their attacking power.

So management had put a couple of real flyers in as loose forwards. Neither was that big, but they could run hard and tackle even harder, courtesy of a league background. Their mission was to hound the shit out of the opposition backs and make their life as miserable and error-ridden as possible.

The coach and manager were experienced in both soldiering and rugby. They had served overseas in various war zones and had played rugby until well into their 40s, when the injuries began to mount. At that stage, they were virtually ordered to stop by the Squadron commander, not wanting such experienced senior NCOs unavailable because of something as mundane as rugby injuries.

At some stage of his career, Staff Heta had also had most of two fingers and half of another blown off his right hand. But the injury never seemed to affect his performance, either as a soldier or on the rugby field. In fact, both were well known as hard, uncompromising men ideal in whatever role they were carrying out. When they spoke, people listened, and so it was at the pre-game pep talk. The players were all ears.

"Run them, run them hard, get those big forwards blowing and tackle them. Tackle them early, tackle them late, I don't care. Put in some big hits early and let them know you're there and you're going to be in their face all day. They've got some quick backs, so you'll have to try and starve them of the ball. But knock them over first time, don't give them any chances. If you get them into a ruck, make sure they know they've been there and they won't want another taste."

Bob Michaels stopped and looked hard at his team for 10 long seconds. "Any questions? Nothing? Well, that's about it then. You got anything to add, Staff?"

"You've about said it all, Bob," replied Staff Heta. "Well, there is one thing. They think they've got it this year because we're short-handed, and we are. For once we're the underdogs, so let's just go out there and show them that these underdogs can bite, okay?" The team all nodded assent. "Okay, let's do it then." The pumped-up team filed eagerly out to do battle.

The first half was an absolute cracker. The plan to run the Gunners forwards to tire them out had worked to a certain extent, but had been negated somewhat by the big-kicking opposition first-five. Apparently he was a new posting, so he had come as a bit of a surprise to the Squadron boys. Every time they got hot on attack and lost the ball, they would suddenly find themselves back in their own 22 desperately defending again. The big men were running all right, but generally it was forward, not backward.

The Gunners scored first and missed the conversion. But they soon slotted a penalty. Right on the stroke of half time, when on desperate defence, one of the Squadron loose forward fliers got an intercept and scored under the bar for an easy conversion, making it 8-7 at the break.

Staff Heta was speaking urgently to his team. "The tactics are working, fellas," he said. "But you've got to hang on to the ball up their end, otherwise that first-five is going to kick it back downfield all day. Fuck's sake, hang on to it and try to not get isolated. That's where you're losing it. You wings, drop back a bit further when it's their ball to help the fullback out. Loosies, get a big one into that first, shorten him up a bit. I know he's standing deep, but you can even make it a bit late if necessary – only in their half, though. Don't want to give away an easy three points."

He continued: "You guys can do it, you know. Look at their big men. They're all lying on the ground. They're stuffed. They'll probably change some of them over at some stage, but they've played their best pack first." He paused and looked at his troops. "Now get out there and give it to them! Any questions? None? Good. Bob?"

"Thanks Staff. This is where your fitness is going to pay off, guys. Keep them running and they'll drop off. Then the holes will begin to open up. Away you go, and good luck."

Twenty-five minutes, three fights and four injury substitutions later, the score was still the same. The game had see-sawed up and down the field. But as in the first half, the Squadron would be hot on attack, lose control of the ball and bang, suddenly back down into their own 22 with it all to do again.

Both teams had had shots at goal but neither team could buy a penalty or score a try. The game was going to go right to the wire, by the look of it, with whoever scoring becoming the hero for their team.

Members of each unit were patrolling up and down the sidelines screaming encouragement, as were the coaches and managers of both teams. It was just about as hectic on the sideline as it was on the field.

The Gunners could sense that perhaps a rare win was on the way and the Squadron was just one score away from maintaining their dominance. Something special was needed. A big ruck in the middle of the field suddenly broke up, leaving one lone figure lying on the ground, motionless. A knock-on and the ref called time off to check on the injured player.

Staff Heta and Bob Michaels charged on. It was one of theirs on the ground, one of the young troopers. He was trying to stand up, but it was obvious he'd had a fair old bash in the head. Legs and head weren't well co-ordinated and he rolled back down to the ground.

"Stay down, Eddie," said Staff Heta.

"I'm all right, I am all right," mumbled Eddie, trying to get up but pinned by Staff Heta's big left hand.

"All right then, how many fingers am I holding up?" Staff Heta extended his digitally challenged right hand. Eddie squinted upwards with some difficulty. "Five," he finally said.

"Get the stretcher, take him to the hospital. He's concussed," Staff Heta ordered. The rest of the team cracked up, never got it back together and the Gunners achieved a rare win.

CIVVY STREET

THE BALACLAVA

"I'm at my wit's end, Bill! Up studying till near midnight and when I do get to bed, he's playing his damn music till all hours of the morning. Then tonight, when Joanne went out to lock the garage, he called her an 'effing C', and that's not proper language for a 15-year-old to be hearing."

Even over the phone, Bill could sense that his sister was near breaking point.

"Have you rung the police or the council noise pollution people tonight?" he asked. He knew the problem had been going on for a while.

"Most of the neighbours have, at one time or another," came the reply. "All he does is turn it down for five minutes or so till they've gone, then turns it straight back up again. And he smokes his bloody wacky baccy on the balcony at night. You can smell it from here. It absolutely reeks."

Bill had a quick think. He really felt sorry for his sister Kath. She'd had a hard time over the past two years or so. Her husband, never much good anyway, had done a runner, leaving her with two teenagers to raise and a mortgage to pay off. She was trying to improve her employment prospects by training to be a teacher while attempting to live on the domestic purposes benefit. Life was tough for her and she certainly didn't need the bullshit her neighbour was giving her.

"Hang in there, kid," he said, using one of their old Mum's favourite sayings. "Is he playing his music at the moment?"

"No, he usually waits till after nine or even later when he knows people will be going to bed," said Kath.

"Okay then, when he starts up, give me a ring. Doesn't matter what time. Ring me. I'll go and have a quiet word with the man and see what I can do. All right?"

"Thanks, Bill," his sister said sadly. "Sorry to bother you with my problems, but I've just about reached the end of my tether. The house won't sell because his overgrown section puts the buyers off. He abused Joanne. It just can't carry on like this." She burst into tears.

Bill was really uncomfortable with that. He hated hearing a woman cry, especially his own sister. "Go back and study and ring me if the music starts up," he said gruffly to hide his feelings.

Kath agreed. Bill headed off home with the beer he had just bought. Back to unexpected guests. His old platoon sergeant, Jerry Ruka, had shown up out of the blue. He was in town visiting his son Marty, a local policeman.

During their reminiscing he had been showing them the mementoes of his 20 years in the army, a lot of them still stored in the steel trunk he had brought back from his first posting to Asia. "To stop the kids from tutuing," was the answer he had given to his wife after one of the kids had asked her why it was always locked.

The phone rang about 11.30pm. It was Kath, not quite in tears but very close to it. "He's playing his music again," she said. "Someone must have rung the council because they've been up already. But no sooner had they gone than the volume was straight back up again."

Bill could sense she was going to carry on, so cut straight in. "All right" he said. "I want you to turn all your lights off. Go to bed and no matter what you might hear, don't turn them on again. Don't even look out the window. I'll go and have a word with this Mr Music, but I don't want him to think you're the one I'm doing it for, okay?"

"Okay. But be careful," Kath said.

"She'll be jake," Bill replied, and put the phone down.

He sat at the kitchen table and had a bit of a think. One thing the army had taught him was that a little bit of preparation and planning could save a hell of a lot of legwork. He could have done without this little bit of drama. But Kath was his sister, the family had always stuck together and one of the last things his mother had said to him before she died was: "Look after the rest of the family, Bill."

So he would do it for his Mum's sake. He was thankful now that he and Jerry hadn't really got into the booze. They had had only a couple each, and Marty hadn't touched it at all. "Couldn't have a drunk copper driving around the place," he laughed.

It was well after midnight when Bill finally went to the garage to get his car. He had decided to wear his black tracksuit. The little bit of camouflage won't go amiss, he thought as he started the car and began to reverse out of the garage. He stopped halfway. The lights shone directly onto the steel army trunk he had opened for Jerry and his son earlier in the day, illuminating his old khaki balaclava left lying out on top.

"Now, that's a good idea," he thought. He jumped out, grabbed it, got back into the car and took off. Parking near the shops about 70 or 80 metres down the road from his sister's house, he began to walk up the road. He placed the balaclava inside the tracksuit top, thinking it would look very suspicious if he were wearing it and a car or pedestrian went by.

There was an alleyway next to Kath's place on the other side of Mr Music. Knowing he could get through the fence and into her place with no problem, he went down it, found the hole, crept round her garage and sat in the shadow where he could observe Mr Music's place without being seen.

Nothing was happening. No music. No noise. Bill sat motionless for more than 10 minutes, just observing and trying to formulate a plan. He finally decided that he would just knock at the door, then take it from there. He was about to move when Mr Music's door opened and a figure stepped onto the balcony, leaned over and lit up a smoke. It was him, all right. Framed by the light of the open door, the lanky frame and long unkempt hair were instantly recognisable. Kath had pointed him out at the shops one day.

Bill couldn't move straight away. He would be seen and he didn't want to be associated with Kath's house in any way. So he just sat and after what seemed like an age, Mr Music began walking down the balcony stairs to the path. Then he headed up towards his letterbox, his back to Bill.

Once out of his direct vision, Bill moved quickly back round the garage into the alley where he paused momentarily to put the balaclava on. Then he crossed the road and walked up until he was opposite Mr Music's house. There, he crossed back over again, again not wanting to be associated with his sister's place.

By this time, Mr Music had turned around and was heading down the path, his back towards him. Bill tiptoed through the slightly opened gate and slipped quietly up behind the man.

"Hey!" he yelled loudly. As the figure stiffened with shock then turned, he grabbed it round the neck with both hands and lifted it bodily off the ground, squeezing ever so gently on the unprotected throat. He then turned the body around and jerked his knee up suddenly, right into the balls. He felt the figure give a sickening grunt, then sag, and he threw it on to the ground.

Placing his foot heavily into the middle of the chest he screamed: "The whole neighbourhood's pissed off with you, mate! You're just a fuckin' arsehole!" He sank a boot fair into the guts, hearing the satisfying "oof" as the air went out of the lungs.

"If I ever hear any more complaints about you, I'll come back and finish the job!" Another boot. "Have you got it?" There was no answer from the cowed, gasping figure. "Have you got it?" Louder this time.

"Yes, yes," came the ragged answer, finally. "Don't fuckin' forget, then! You won't want to be seeing me again, or you'll be dead meat!"

Bill turned and walked quickly up to the letterbox, crossed the road and headed back toward his car, breaking into a mad dash after about 30 metres. He jumped into the car, started it up, adrenaline flowing, completely forgetting about his headwear. He drove home, a different way this time. He parked the car in the garage, closed the door, went inside and jumped into bed fully clothed minus shoes but still wearing the balaclava. He was a bit worried that he might have overdone the violence. Once the adrenaline started flowing, it was a bloody hard thing to control.

After about five minutes' musing he burst out laughing, which woke his missus up. She looked at him quizzically, then said "You're mad," and went straight back to sleep.

Kath rang him the next morning and excitedly said that she had overheard everything. The police had turned up about half an hour later and they had heard him yelling at them. But the real good news was that when she had got back from her course that afternoon, there had been a "for sale" sign on his house.

"That's great," said a slightly relieved Bill. "Don't tell a soul, will you? I didn't really mean to get that heavy. It just happened. I could be charged with assault, you know."

"Don't be silly, Bill. I've already spoken to the kids about it they're sworn to secrecy. You're their hero at the moment, you know. Thanks very much."

"No sweat," said Bill. "But he hasn't gone yet. Let me know if it happens again, will you?"

"I don't really think it will," she replied. "You've frightened him enough to put his house on the market. I think that says it all."

"Hope you're right," said Bill. He didn't really want to have to be doing it all again.

The following morning's local paper carried an account of an early morning assault on a home owner. The only description the victim could give was a tall, solid man dressed in black and wearing a balaclava. Police were investigating but had no leads, the report said.

Later on that evening Bill got an awful fright when, answering a knock at the door, he found Marty, Jerry Ruka's policeman son, standing there. "Kia ora, Bill," he said with a big grin on his face. "Just dropped round with a message from Dad. He said you'd better put that old balaclava back in the trunk and leave it there."

Bill's mouth sagged open as Marty, with an even wider grin, turned and walked back to the police car.

NEVER A TEAM THAT COULDN'T BE BEAT

The coach was growing exasperated. Come on you guys, he thought to himself. Only 10 minutes to kick-off and still five players short. He'd bloody told them he wanted a full turn-out this week. He badly wanted a victory this time, after all the criticism and complaints heaped on them by the opposition team's parents and supporters after last year's clash. Their club was the oldest and most affluent in town, and this team hadn't been beaten for well over two years now. They had a couple of early-season losses as under-13s but had remained unbeaten as under-14s and so far this year as well.

The club made sure this record was well publicised on the local radio and in the paper as well. Mind you, they did have a lot of talent to pick from, with two teams in many grades. They also enjoyed the money, time and effort put in by some high-profile rugby people. There was probably no real excuse for them not doing well.

The coach's own club wasn't so well off financially or membership-wise, being based in a predominantly state housing suburb with high unemployment. A good percentage of the club's junior players were from broken families, living with a solo mum or dad. This generally didn't augur too well in the financial or discipline stakes.

The club was really finding it hard to make ends meet. It would probably have been forced into recess a few years ago if it wasn't for the golden oldies team, for which the coach had played for five years now.

Even the senior team was scratching for decent players. And if they did happen to develop one with excellent potential, the bigger clubs seduced them with offers, promises and jobs. It was difficult to compete with these richer outfits, and in most cases you couldn't really blame the player, either. He was just looking after himself in what were generally pretty difficult economic times.

But it was still frustrating, especially when the club had bought a player right through the junior grades, often with not too much parental support, financial or otherwise. In fact, it was always difficult to win support from parents, whether it be just paying the fees (which weren't exorbitant by any stretch of the imagination), turning up regularly to barrack for the team, or helping with transport to outlying country clubs

He remembered back to earlier in the year when they'd had to travel nearly 40 miles for a game in the country, and he'd found himself stone motherless in the club car park with no parents and 14 players to somehow fit into his Toyota LiteAce.

He'd got 'em all in all right – squashed all over the place: On the floor, in the back, one on top of the other. Anywhere that could possibly fit a body, he'd put one there. Highly illegal, of course, and if they'd had an accident or been stopped by a cop, he'd have probably gone for a row of shit- cans. But fortunately they'd got there safely, only to discover the missing 15th player already there, along with his mother in an otherwise empty car that could have taken at least four other players.

It was a frustrating task at times but with his love of rugby, he persevered. He'd been coaching most of these boys for some five years now. Several showed exceptional promise but lacked the necessary discipline or motivation to take that extra step upwards. A few were in and out of trouble constantly, at home, at school or on the street. Sometimes they disappeared completely for days on end. The police were regular callers at his training sessions, knowing that was one place where they might catch up with whoever happened to be in trouble or was missing.

Earlier that year, just before practice one afternoon, he'd actually caught a couple of them smoking marijuana. He kicked both their arses, threatened them with the police and flushed the shit down the toilet. But he was well aware that in reality, it was only the tip of the iceberg.

One of his best players was still under the guidance of the Justice Department for burglary and vandalism, while several others awaited police action on the same or similar offences.

Even his own son, Matt, had got into the shit the previous year, having to front up to the Children's Court after having been caught wearing a stolen designer T-shirt. He'd been given it by one of the other members of the team, and as a lot of other gear had gone missing at the same time as the T-shirt and he wouldn't say who had given it to him, he'd had to carry the can for the lot.

His punishment was community service, to be overseen and administered by the president of the club. So Matt found himself club groundsman and odd-job man for the season, an appointment that successfully took up all of his Saturdays and a fair few Sundays as well. Lesson learnt there. He missed his weekends off something chronic and would hopefully look a gift horse in the mouth in future.

The team was actually quite family-orientated, with numerous cousins and two sets of brothers. One lot were twins, while the others were unusual in that the younger brother was bigger than his sibling who was 10 months older. The rest of the team soon nicknamed them Big Little and Little Big. They were both excellent players, though, and because the younger one was so big and heavy, he'd been forced to play up a grade every year.

He remembered when the two first turned up to training from out of the blue a few years back, having just moved into the area. Their mouths just wouldn't stay shut while he was trying to coach and finally, in desperation, he kicked both their arses and sent them home, telling them to come back when they found some manners.

Big Little had cried and said that his father would come back and punch the coach in the head. Send him over, the coach replied, and once I tell him what you've been doing, he'll probably kick your arse as well. Well, the father hadn't fronted and when the coach finally met him some weeks later, he knew nothing about the incident.

Each year, half a dozen or so of his boys were selected for the rep trials. But usually, few even bothered to turn up. Or if they did, they gave the selector too much lip and got sent home early. The coach had had cured them of giving him lip, though. They all knew what would happen if they did. It was an old and favourite technique: He'd make them practise kick-offs to him, and he'd pick out the mouthy ones and run straight at them, forcing them to tackle him properly, get knocked arse over turkey or avoid him altogether. If they did chicken out and dodge him, their mates would give them that much shit that it was never regarded an option.

Generally speaking he had them worked out. If only they'd listen. All they needed to do was all turn up, listen to the referee, play the game, and not fight, and they had the beating of any team in the competition. But they never seemed to be able do all of those things at once. If he had a full team, some would end up in the sin bin or sent off for the rest of the game, or they'd give the ref some lip and turn him against them for the rest of the game. But usually, they'd just decide it was a good day for a fight. It was a standing joke between him and some of the other coaches. "Are your boys going to fight or play today?" they'd ask. He'd just shrug and look up at the sky, because he never knew himself what was going to occur. Each and every Saturday was as big a mystery to him as anyone else. But there was no mistake that most of the other teams feared or respected his rough, tough and rugged team, mostly Maori boys with a few battle-hardened pakeha thrown in for good measure. They had talent to burn. But unfortunately, they seldom chose to make the best use of it.

Snapping out of his reverie, he looked around the park again. It was chocker with spectators and more were arriving. All supporting the other team. of course. Must have been at least 200 – mums, dads, brothers, sisters and club members. Mind you it was their home game, so there should be good support.

His only regular supporter was the only one who'd turned up so far today. Old faithful Charlie had come to watch his son and nephew play. At least those two always turned up on time. He heard yelling, turned and was pleased to see his missing players strolling nonchalantly onto the park. Charlie was bellowing: "Come on, you guys, you're slower than my old Auntie Huia. Get your A into G."

The rest of the team laughed at the latecomers and the coach checked his watch again. Less than five minutes to go and he still had to give the team sheet to the ref. But at least he had a full list today. He hurriedly filled it in, and gave it to the younger brother of one of his players to deliver to the ref, and called his boys in for the team talk.

"Listen up, you guys," he said. But the chattering continued. "Listen up!" he yelled. Charlie circled around behind them, ready to clip an ear and shut a mouth if he thought it necessary.

"This is one game we really want to win," the coach said. "I'm sick of all the mouthing off they do, and I know you are too. I reckon we were robbed in the return game last year, with that fill-in ref being one of their own club members. You can do it! You have the talent! All you've got to do is play the game! Don't fight! Don't mouth off at the ref! Just play your natural game!" the coach exhorted his players.

"You forwards, I want to see you sticking together like shit to a blanket and driving hard into those rucks and mauls. You loosies, get in amongst that back line, hound the shit out of them, knock 'em over, make their lives a complete misery, and most of all, back the bloody backs up! You inside backs, for Christ's sake, catch and spin the ball! You've got a quick, fast centre and wings out there! For God's sake, use them! Give them good clean ball, and they'll get you the tries!" He stopped dramatically and glared at them all. "Okay, is everybody clear?" There was no answer. "Is everybody clear!" he repeated, louder this time. "Yes!" they all yelled together.

"Good," he said. "Oh, and one last thing before you go on: What did Confucius say?" They all laughed, knowing what was coming. "Well? What did he say? Dan, you tell us."

He always asked Daniel, who answered in very passable Chinese-accented English: "Ah, glasshopper, man without legs find it very difficult to run crick." They all laughed again.

"And what does that mean?" the coach demanded. From down the back came a muffled reply. "Say it again, louder this time!" the coach demanded. The voice grew clearer: "Tackle."

"Right, so what are we going to do all day?" the coach asked. "TACKLE!" the players called in unison. "Say it again three times," the coach demanded. "TACKLE, TACKLE, TACKLE," came the chant.

"Right, now get out there and do it! Play your natural game and you'll win! Listen to your captain and the ref and you'll win! And the biggest thing to remember: Keep your bloody mouths shut!"

He threw the ball to the captain, a big rangy Maori boy who ate like a bloody horse but never got fat, just as the ref blew his whistle. "Okay Troy, take 'em out. Good luck, boys!" The coach headed up to the halfway mark, reasonably satisfied because at least they had a full team. That was a positive start.

The crowd had grown even larger. The car park was pretty full and the home club's netball teams were leading the encouragement as the teams ran on. At least we've got a neutral ref this time, the coach thought as he looked around. Apart from him and Charlie, and a couple of younger brothers who filled in as the reserves after their own games, there was no one else to cheer his team on.

Come on guys, you can do it, give us a big one for once, he said to himself, then aloud to Charlie, "Whata ya think, mate?"

Charlie, who always had a smile on his face despite a sometimes tenuous existence in and out of employment, laughed. "Do 'em like a dog's dinner, I reckon," he said.

"Wish I had your confidence," came the reply.

"We're overdue for the big one, eh boy?" said Charlie, giving the thumbs up. "And I reckon this is it."

"Hope you're right," said the coach. Then a mighty roar erupted from the expectant, excited and extremely partisan crowd. The game had begun.

The first 10 minutes were pretty even, the game ebbing and flowing with neither side taking any clear advantage. His forwards were working well, driving the ball up. But when they turned over, the opposition's big-kicking first-five would drive them way back down field and they would have to start all over again. But they were tackling anything that moved, hard and low, making the opposing backs think hard about crashing it up. They seemed to be listening to the ref and to Troy, who was generally a dependable and unflappable good influence on most, although not all, of them.

The opposition suddenly launched an attack, with their backs spinning it wide. But his backs were equal to the occasion and tackled beautifully, the loosies on the spot and scavenging for the ball. The opposition winger was been crashed to the ground after receiving a bit of a hospital pass from his equally hammered centre. But he took exception to the tackle and wouldn't let the ball go. Just as the ref blew his whistle to award a penalty, the coach groaned as Joe, his team's winger, smacked his opposite in the mouth, right in front of the ref. Joe was a real flyer on the field, probably because he was constantly running away from the trouble he got into at home and at school.

The crowd bayed as the ref blew his whistle sharply again, called Joe over, then pointed to the sideline. The coach hung his head as the crowd erupted delightedly. Christ, not even the sin bin, just straight off. Makes it bloody hard now.

Troy yelled at him, asking what to do. "Don't replace Joe on the wing!" the coach yelled. "The forwards are going well enough. Tell the blindside loosie and the half to cover it. Use the forwards! Keep it tight! Hit it up! Hit it up!"

The coach caught the eye of his son Matt, playing halfback, and nodded. Matt knew what to do, all right. If there was one thing that bugger could to besides model designer fucking T-shirts, it was tackle.

Smashing it up the middle was the only way his boys were going to win now. They were good at it, too, if only they could get it going. Suck the opposition into a forward battle and sap their energy, and if they could cover that gap, they just might still have a chance. The game resumed with the coach and Charlie both watching a little despondently. Realistically, it was more than a hard ask now.

Fifteen minutes later, their spirits had risen considerably. The game remained scoreless and his boys were definitely holding their own, although the forwards weren't quite as dominant as he would have liked.

Suddenly something quite inexplicable happened. Little Big, who seemed to be fired up about something, made a crashing burst up into the opposition's 22, running right through a couple of would-be tacklers on the way. When he was finally held up, he was still on his feet with a couple of loosies plus Big Little right up his arse, and they drove him on an angle towards the try line and the corner flag.

It was a toss-up which one they'd get to first. Then Troy arrived and, thinking quickly as ever, started driving the ruck back infield, enlisting the sole winger's assistance as well. They drove the maul over the try line, where it collapsed to the ground. Then Little Big stood up triumphantly, ball still in hand. The ref had no hesitation in awarding the try, in the face of disagreement from spectators who loudly asked how the hell he could see what happened. Too late, though, the points were on the board. The kick from out wide was missed. Shock, horror, though, it was 5-0 to the unfancied.

The crowd roared out advice to their own team: Don't worry! There's only 14 of them! They'll crack! They haven't got the discipline! Plenty of time! You'll win! You'll win! In their minds, the try against their team just an aberration and victory was virtually assured.

But the coach could see that for once, the boys were doing something right. They had their tails up and they weren't listening to any of that shit. They claimed the kick-off cleanly and started driving back down towards the enemy line in classic style. Smashing it up, turning when stopped and giving it to the next one . . . once they got into the rhythm and got the roll on, they were near unstoppable.

Somewhere in among it all, the ref detected a small knock-on. Scrum down, opposition put-in. The boys went down still fired up, timed the push brilliantly, back-pedalled the opposition scrum and claimed a tighthead. Not really expecting the ball, Matt had a sudden rush of blood to the head and made a dab round the blind side, away from his own support.

There was no one home except the opposition winger, because they'd been expecting the ball and had a planned move ready, with their fullback out in midfield. Matt ran straight at the winger, sold an outrageous dummy to the missing Joe (who was actually standing on the sideline near halfway), then set sail for the line half the field away. The coach knew Matt was very quick over 20 or 30 metres or so. But he was no out-and-out speedster and as the opposition fullback gradually closed in and lined up the tackle, he mentally urged Matt to kick and chase.

Then suddenly a tall thin dark figure loomed up inside Matt from the other side of the field. It was Dan, the running man – the fastest runner in the team and possibly the whole competition. Matt shimmied and made to kick, and the coach thought for an instant he hadn't seen Dan. But then he drew the fullback in and threw the pass as he was crashed to the ground. It wasn't the greatest pass ever but Dan caught it and galloped clear. It was good night, nurse. No one was going to catch him from there. Under the sticks. The unhappy crowd roared: What about the forward pass? Line ball, the ref ruled. Too late, anyway. The points were awarded and the kick was a mere formality. More horror for the home supporters to digest: 12-0 to the unfancied. Still a long way from the end, though.

The boys were now fired right up. The forwards had gained ascendancy over the opposition pack and were firing on all cylinders, while the backs were doing their job. It was almost as if they felt they had nothing to lose and might as well give it their best shot.

The kick-off was a long one, almost predictably down to the vacant winger's spot. The fullback called, caught it, shaped to kick for safety then suddenly pinned his ears back and went down the line like a runaway train taking everyone by surprise, even his own team. He easily beat the few forwards who'd chased the kick up and ran straight at the wing who'd hung back for the clearing kick.

Just when it looked like he was going to try and crunch him, that tall dark figure was there again calling urgently for the ball. Mad Dan on the burst again. The fullback drew the opposing winger and flicked the pass. It was a shocker, only knee high. That's the end of that, the coach thought.

But Dan slowed, bent and picked it up then pinned his ears back again and away he went. He ran straight at the opposing fullback in mid field, stopping him dead in his tracks. Then about two metres away, he swerved sharply and headed for the corner. It worked. The fullback had stopped completely and had no chance against Dan's pace. He was cleanly beaten, left sprawled on the ground. Dan then headed back infield to score under the sticks.

The coach and Charlie were cock-a-hoop. "Hoo-wee! They're never going to catch that boy from behind!" Charlie yelled. "He's got too much gas!" The crowd was noticeably quieter, stunned by the three quick tries. The kick went over and it was now 19-0 to the unfancied with just over five minutes to halftime.

If we can keep them out until halftime, we've got a real chance, the coach thought. "Play the line! Play the line!" he yelled to the first-five, Troy and Matt. "Keep it in their half!" But his boys were never ones to listen much. They had other ideas. The forwards, aided by a lacklustre follow-up from the opposition, fielded the kick and immediately started hitting it up, relentlessly and remorselessly grinding their way back up the field again.

They reached the 22 in centre field before they were held up when the maul collapsed, turning it into a ruck. As the ball was slowly cleared back to Matt, the ref blew his whistle and awarded them a penalty. One of the opposition backs was offside. It was easily kickable and the crowd groaned while the coach yelled: "Take the shot! Take the shot!" But Matt had other ideas. He tapped it quickly and ran with a pack of hungry forwards right up his arse. He got dumped but turned and presented the ball to Troy, who picked it up and charged straight, turning before getting tackled and handing it to Little Big, who put his head down and set sail. The rest of the forwards got behind and they drove him over for his second try just to the right of the posts. The ref hesitated only momentarily before awarding the try.

Charlie was ecstatic. "Shit, 24 bloody nil," he said. But it was soon 26-0 and the huge home crowd was uncharacteristically silent as the halftime whistle went.

The coach led his team right into the middle of the field, as far away as possible from the crowd and any eavesdroppers. There'd been complaints in the past about the way he spoke to the boys. Outsiders took it literally when they heard his instructions to "smash your opposite number or line 'em up and knock 'em down". He'd been accused of advocating violence when all he was doing was using language the boys would understand.

They congregated in the middle of the field and as the water bottles were being chucked around, the boys talked non-stop, absolutely delighted with their first half.

"Shut up, you guys!" the coach yelled. "Listen up!" Once again, Charlie circled behind the boys, playing the role of enforcer. He was bloody good at that.

"Okay," the coach said. "You've had a bloody good first half. They took you too easy after Joe got sent off and you surprised the hell out of them. You've got a handy lead, but believe me, the second half isn't going to be quite so easy. So shut up, suck it in and listen. You'll still need all your wind to win this one. It ain't in the bag yet."

He paused for a few seconds and looked at all the happy faces. "They're going to use their backs this half to try and take advantage of that overlap, you can be sure of that. When we're in their half, we'll keep the eight forwards intact. Keep it tight and hit it up. They don't seem to appreciate that. But when we're on defence, Josh," he said, pointing at the number eight, "you cover the vacant wing spot."

Josh groaned. Forwards generally didn't like acting as backs. "It's an important job, Josh," the coach said. "And if we want to win this game, it has to be done." He looked intensely at Josh until he was sure the message was understood.

"Now," he said, addressing the forwards. "What you've got to do is drive it up, drive it up and suck all the energy out of their forwards till we get on to the attack. You backs, it's tackle, tackle, tackle this half. Target the ball and try and smother it so they can't get it back. It'll slow things down and eat up the time and we might just get the scrum. Don't worry if they get the odd try or two, it's bound to happen. Just don't toss it away, that's all I ask. You can win this one! It's a big ask, but you can do it!"

He stopped and looked at each boy, then asked: "Any questions?" There were a couple of queries which he answered, then he and Charlie went around each player exhorting and encouraging them until the whistle went.

"Good luck, boys!" he and Charlie yelled as they filed out. Forty long minutes to go. The coach suddenly realised he hadn't mentioned discipline once during the halftime break, which was highly unusual. But there hadn't been a problem after Joe had been sent off and it was probably better not to tempt fate anyway.

The crowd had found its voice and was fired up again. All the usual advice rang out: They'll crack! They've got no discipline! You're the better team!

There were also racist taunts. But fortunately his boys weren't listening. They were still high on adrenaline, which was just as bloody well. Charlie heard it, though. But all he did was look hard at the culprits and point to the scoreboard, which was just as well. They wouldn't want to upset Charlie. He could go right off and be very hard to stop. The coach looked at the scoreboard, too, and thought it would be real good if it stayed like that.

The second half kicked off and the battle raged up and down the field. His forwards generally gave better than they got, but every time they got on to the attack, they seemed to make a mistake. This allowed the opposition to clear the ball away with their big-kicking first-five or, more often than not, their backs. They were trying to take advantage of the overlap, obviously to instructions. However, it was still 17 minutes before they got their first try, under the bar and converted, which certainly made the crowd wake up a bit.

The coach grew worried. His boys seemed tired and in some disarray, and it was only another five minutes or so before they conceded another try, near the corner this time. But it was converted with an excellent kick to make the scoreline 26-14 and the game not nearly over yet. The crowd was definitely awake now. Another converted try and they were within range. Troy rallied the troops and Charlie and the coach yelled themselves hoarse above the noise of the spectators.

His team was hot on attack when the worst thing happened. Matt threw a silly, under-pressure pass from an unexpected ball. The opposition second-five, very probably off side, intercepted it and set sail for the line. Dan chased valiantly but just missed. The opposing player had had too much of a start. He scored under the sticks and the conversion went over easily. The crowd was baying. With the score at 21- 26, victory was in sight.

The coach looked at his watch. Just under a quarter of an hour to go. He didn't much fancy their chances of hanging on. Charlie was yelling, "Kia kaha! Kia kaha!" as the game restarted to the home crowd's partisan roar.

His boys were definitely tiring. Being short of one man for most of the game was now taking its toll and they spent the next 10 minutes on desperate defence before finally and almost inevitably conceding another try. It was converted, to the shrill satisfaction of the home crowd. All was well. The politically and morally correct team was now in front of the unfancied, almost detestable, team. With less than five minutes to go, they were now up 28-26. They looked unbeatable.

They surged with new confidence back on to the attack and only desperate tackling denied them yet another try. The boys hung on grimly, mostly out on their feet, and the coach began mentally conceding the game. The ref reinforced the feeling by penalising them centrefield midway between their 22 and half way.

The opposition's first-five ignored the advice to have a shot, which probably would have taken them to full time. Instead, he tapped it and ran. As he got close to the defence, he threw a flat pass to one of his forwards who had followed him up. And that was just what Matt was waiting for. Having given up an intercept pass and try himself, he desperately wanted revenge. Very quick off the mark and possibly half a yard offside, he sliced between the first-five and the forward, gratefully accepted the ball, pinned his ears back and away he went. An immediate roar came up from the crowd: Off side! Off side! But the ref obviously thought otherwise and let the play go on.

Matt still had work to do. He'd caught them by surprise but there were still players near him, chasing hard and slowly gathering him in. Directly in front of him was the fullback, lining him up and waiting. He'd just decided to chip over the top when he heard the call and looked to his right. It was the running Dan, having a screaming blinder, about five yards behind but travelling. Matt knew he was being chased and hoped he could just make it to the fullback before they got him. He desperately put in a spurt.

The tackle came in from behind and Charlie and the coach groaned, thinking Matt hadn't seen Dan. But it wasn't over. As he fell, Matt had kept his hands free and got the pass away. Not what you'd call a brilliant one – more of a lob than anything else. But it arced up, then dropped right into Dan's clutching fingers. Like a lot of speedsters, he was usually butter-fingered. But today his hands had glue on.

Dan went off on a burst and no one on that field could touch him. He galloped clear, grounded the ball under the bar then dropped, totally winded. It had been a long run at full pace.

There was a stunned silence then both Charlie and the coach erupted. "You fucking beauty!" yelled Charlie, completely forgetting the presence of women and children. A couple of the boys had enough energy to run down and congratulate Dan, while the rest slapped Matt on the back at halfway. Troy told the fullback to take his time with the kick, which he did. They'd had enough for that day.

The opposing coach went round to the dead ball line to talk to his team. He told them not to worry, they hadn't lost because their opposition had unregistered and overweight players. The result wouldn't stand. The kick went over to the cheers of the coach and Charlie. The ref immediately looked at his watch and blew full time. A big upset – the unfancied and almost despised team won 33-28. The boys were absolutely knackered and just sat on the ground at halfway with big smiles all over their faces.

They all knew they had just done something very special. The opposing coach was still at it, complaining bitterly to the ref. But the ref stood firm. As far as he was concerned, the result stood and if the coach had any complaint, he should take it up with the committee. He did want Joe's name for the judiciary, though.

Getting no joy from the ref, the opposing coach then approached the winning team, telling them not to celebrate too much because they hadn't won and the result would be reversed. When Charlie suggested that he was just a bad sportsman and if he didn't fuck off he'd be dropped, the chap beat a hasty retreat, although still making all sorts of threats. The crowd was disappearing fast, thwarted and disappointed, although a knot of parents and players remained on the field with someone gesticulating madly and pointing their way.

But the boys still sat exhausted, most not even bothering to talk. It was the quietest the coach had ever known them to be. "No matter what happens from here," he said, "you won the game and I'm proud of you. You beat the team that couldn't be beat and with 14 men. Player of the day today is..." he hesitated "...the whole team, and if you can find enough energy to move, I'll shout you all at McDonald's. Even you, Joe."

He looked hard at his errant winger. "You and I will have to front up to the judiciary on Wednesday night. Just make sure you turn up. I'll ring you with the time."

That got them all moving and as they slowly and happily trudged off to where their gear was, Troy was ecstatic and whooping. "We beat the bastards! We beat the bastards!" he kept saying. They sure did, although the coach was worried about how he would explain to his wife about the money he was spending at McDonald's. But caught up in the moment, he dismissed it from his mind. We'll cross that bridge when we come to it, he thought.

As expected, the opposition did put in a protest. They alleged that the coach had unregistered players and overweight players. They complained about the referee. They grumbled about anything they could think of. After the judicial hearing on Wednesday night, the coach was called upon to address the allegations. He'd done his homework and had his reply ready.

Yes he did have three unregistered players, he said. They hadn't attended on opening day, so they weren't weighed in. He had since tried three times to get them weighed in but there had been no scales available at the base ground each time they had played there. He had, however, included them on every team sheet when they'd played. And they were within the weight limit because he'd had them weighed at the club, and had a signed statement from a Junior Management Board member to bear this out.

Once this had been sighted and accepted, he then admitted that he did have one overweight player. But he pointed out that this player should have been playing for the under-14s but was too heavy. He then produced a copy of the board's own rules which stated that overweight players could only have to play up one age group. When they wrote that one, they probably didn't think a kid might be too heavy for the age group above him. After that he was asked to retire while the committee considered its decision. Of course he didn't mention all the frantic running around he'd done since the game, organising the unregistered boys to be weighed in and witnessed by a sympathetic committee member, and double checking on Big Little's birth date.

It was only 10 short minutes before he was called back in, which made him feel quite optimistic. And so it proved. The committee's decision was that as long as the unregistered boys weighed in under the allowable weight, the result should stand, and he was quite right about the younger boy only having to play up one grade. With the hearing ended just about the whole committee congratulated him on the result. It seemed he wasn't the only one getting sick of a certain club's constant crowing.

The team finished fourth in the competition that year, with three players making the reps. There were lots of congratulatory messages from other clubs, mainly the smaller and struggling ones. It seemed the coach's boys had shown the others the way, too, as the previously unbeaten team were done twice more that year.

The coach also received offers from several of the larger clubs. But he turned them down. He liked his boys, even though there were ratbags and trouble-makers among them. He understood them and sometimes he could even get the best out of them. He liked to think that perhaps he was something positive and constant in their sometimes turbulent lives. And anyway, if he didn't coach them, who the hell else would?

It was a pity, he thought, that the big clubs used their prosperity and affluence to attract the more promising players away from the small, struggling clubs. If some of these clubs were forced to close, a percentage of their players would certainly be lost, to the detriment of themselves and the game. And that would be a pity and a sure crime, he thought. There must be some way of ensuring this did not occur. Surely all kids deserve an equal opportunity, not just the ones from rich clubs.

GIVE THE DOG A BONE

"Jayz, that dog of yours can jump, boy," said Jock.

"Yeah, I know," Mac replied. "But the trouble is that it's got me in the shit with the council. I've been fined twice because he gets out and roams when I'm not here, the bugger."

Jock laughed. "I saw them trying to catch him last week. They had a rope on a pole trying to get it over his neck, but he was too smart for them. He'd let them get so close, then duck away. It was quite funny to watch and they were fair getting pissed off. Eventually I came over and opened the gate. He went in like a lamb and you should have seen their faces. But I mean, your fence is, what, eight foot tall? It's not your fault if the bloody dog is an acrobat and can get over it."

"The trouble is, they don't see it like that, Jock," said Mac. "They said to put him on a chain, which I did, and he fuckin' hated it. He chewed through it in two days' flat. They reckon if I can't control him, he may have to be put down."

"A bit harsh, I'd have thought," said Jock. "You need a dog round the house if you're out all day, with what goes on these days. Millie and I are lucky because we're usually at home all day."

The subject of their discussion gazed adoringly up at his master from his lying position. Blade was a three-year-old blue heeler with bright brown eyes, piercing and intelligent, and a coat that was a variety of shades of grey right through to black. A strict one-man dog, he only really took any notice of his master. In his canine mind, anyone else was just another pair of ankles to be nipped if he could sneak in close enough.

He was as cunning as the proverbial water-closet rodent, too. He wasn't really a barker, and a stranger seeing him approach would think him friendly because he seemed to have a grin on his face, almost as though he thought life was a just a joke. But the joke was always on someone else. He would sidle around behind his unsuspecting victim to see if there was a chance for a bit of a nip. If you had bare feet or wore jandals or sandals, and weren't quick enough, you were in real peril.

And could he jump . . . what a jumper! Mac had seen him jump back into the yard one day. No run-up, no nothing. He'd just eyed up the top of the fence and bang. He'd get his front paws over the top and use the back ones to claw his way over. Mac reckoned he could probably jump 10 or 12 feet if he had to, so it would probably do no good making the fence any taller. It was a worry to Mac, though. He loved his dog and didn't want him put down. But he couldn't afford to keep paying the bloody fines, either.

The problem had begun when Mac got a new job that involved travelling to other towns, sometimes being away for two or three nights at a time. He'd not long moved in with his sister Tracy, who'd ditched her live-in boyfriend and needed help with the rent. The house had a nice big backyard that looked ideal for the dog, so Mac hadn't needed too much convincing. There were no problems with Blade when Mac was working locally and coming home every night. Man and dog would walk the local park morning and night. But now Blade was taking himself for the walk when Mac was away.

The dog only just tolerated Tracy, too. It looked at her with utter disdain if she called him and refused to let her put him on the chain. When she fed it, it would approach the food only after she walked away. He was becoming a real problem dog, old Blade. As neighbours go, you'd have to say that Jock was one of the best. He and Millie, both in their 70s, lived over the road and were forever out in their garden. A few giddays had led to conversations and finally Millie invited Tracy in for a cup of tea.

She walked into the lounge and was utterly surprised to see a photo of her Dad and Jock on the wall. They'd been in the army together, shared a tour overseas and thought the world of each other. Jock had emigrated as a teenager, apparently from a really rough area in Glasgow where he'd learned to take care of himself at an early age. His accent had all but disappeared over the years but their Dad reckoned that when he got excited, he'd revert back to it. He also said of Jock that although there wasn't much of him, there wasn't a scared bone in his body and he'd charge hell with a water pistol and a full bladder.

Jock had muttered something about their Dad being a hard man himself and there had been some talk about the two having a bit of a get-together, although it hadn't eventuated as yet. Their Dad, who was seven or so years younger than Jock, lived in another town and was still working. But it certainly was good having someone friendly living close by, although Tracy had discovered that once she got cornered by Millie, it was quite hard to get away. This made Mac laugh when she'd told him. "You know why women usually knit when they gossip, don't you?" he'd asked her. "To give them something to think about." A cushion had come flying across the room.

"How long are you going away for this week?" asked Jock. "Three nights," replied Mac. "Away Monday, back Thursday." It was a wet Sunday afternoon and Jock had invited them over for the happy hour, which he seemed to have every day about four o'clock.

Tracy had been invited, too, but had cried off with toothache. "The poor wee lamb," Millie had exclaimed when Mac had told her that Tracy had an infected ingrown wisdom tooth and wouldn't be able to have it out until the infection had subsided.

"That poor wee lamb is at home in bed swallowing brandy, chewing painkillers and penicillin and exhibiting all the temperament of a suddenly awoken hibernating snake," Mac had laughingly replied. He'd once heard his father use that description for an officer he'd served under.

"Still, she's your sister. Do you not feel sorry for her?" Millie chided. Brothers and sisters often fight with and disparage each other, but generally if anyone else does it, they immediately join forces. And so it was with these two.

"She's big enough and ugly enough to look after herself," Mac said. "It's been playing up for ages and she should have gone to the dentist yonks ago." Millie shook her head sorrowfully.

"Anyway I'll keep an eye on the place while you're away" said Jock. "There's been a bloody gang of hoodlums going round doing daylight burglaries while people are at work. They've been spotted by a couple of people who didn't actually realise what was going on. They reckon they're all young and wear sunglasses and hoodies. Probably those idiots you see hanging round the mall, crutch of their pants hanging down by their knees, have to hang on to them to keep 'em up. They dunno how ridiculous they look. Lazy young sods. I'd like to get them into the army. They wouldn't know what hit 'em."

"Don't get started on that again, Jock," said Millie. "Those days are long gone now. No more CMT or National Service, more's the pity. But you are right, though. They've bent over so far backwards with the discipline, there just doesn't seem to be any these days."

"Damn right I'm right!" Jock was warming up now. "There's too many feathery-legged, tree-hugging, kissy-kissy, sancti-fuckin'-monious, spare-the-rod, god-bothering idiots in Parliament for my liking."

Millie clicked her tongue at the profanities and Mac laughed because he'd often heard his father utter something decidedly similar.

"You're probably right," he said. "Anyway, thanks for keeping an eye on the place, and the drinks. I better get off and see if the snake's in a better frame of mind. Cheers."

"No worries," said Jock. "If I see something amiss, I'll get on to it quick smart. You know, with all the shit going on these days, it almost makes me wish I had a crowd-pleaser in the house. That would sort anybody out, for sure."

Mac hadn't heard that expression before. "What the hell's that?"

"It's a bloody sawn-off shotgun, a top weapon for controlling a crowd because there's enough for everybody." Mac and Jock laughed while Millie just clicked her tongue again.

"You're bad enough without a weapon, old man," she said. "Honestly, Mac, you want to see him, up and down to the front window like a caged ferret keeping an eye on things. When are you going to learn? You're old, you're past it, you old fool."

"The weapon doesn't know how old the finger is that squeezes the wee titty, old lady," was the rejoinder. And away at it they went. Mac took his opportunity and slipped out the door, leaving them to it.

He smiled to himself. Old Jock was just like their Dad, all right. He recalled the time a few years ago when Tracy had been followed by a couple of guys while coming home from a late shift at work. On the verge of hysterics, she'd rung Dad on her mobile. He'd immediately yelled to Mac and the two had sped off down the road. They had arrived just as the two had bailed Tracy up.

Dad had leapt out of the car and charged straight at them, screaming like hell. They scarpered, with him hot on their trail. They were bloody lucky to have darkness and youth on their side, and they managed to get away. If he'd caught them, who knows what might have happened? He turned up about a quarter of an hour later, totally out of breath and very, very angry.

Tracy had shed tears of relief when they got home and Dad had sat both down and given them a stern lecture. "When you get cornered in a situation like that and you think you're in danger, or anyone else for that matter, that's when you have to remember the old infantryman's adage," he said. "Attack is always the best means of defence. You have to get downright mean and dirty, turn on them with blood in the eye and cloud over the brain and fuckin' give it to them.

"You yell scream, bite, scratch, go for the balls, do anything you can to hurt them," he continued. "And don't worry about it, just hurt the fuck out of them. Always remember, they were probably going to do the same to you if they could. A lot of those sort of people are only brave in a group and if all of a sudden they find themselves being attacked instead, they're liable to find the odds not to their liking and cut and run. Lastly, never ever give up. Do what you have to do to get out of it. You owe it to yourself."

He stared at them for 30 or so long seconds. "Do you understand?" They both nodded. "Good," he said. "Hopefully it'll never ever come to that, but you never know." Then he gave Tracy a cuddle, which was a very rare act for him. A couple of days later he'd handed her a medium-sized pocket-knife to carry in her purse. "Just in case," he'd said. When she looked at it later, she saw it had been well sharpened.

Mac had never forgotten his Dad's advice and although he'd never found himself in any sort of situation, he did keep his school-days cricket bat close to the door of their house "just in case", as he'd repeated to Tracy when he moved in. The bat was rather uncharitably christened "Ollie the equalizer". It was named after Olive, a battle-axe of a woman with a very good heart who'd been their childhood neighbour. She'd given the family wonderful support after their mother had died.

Ollie had been Tracy and Mac's go-to woman when they were army brats whose Dad was often away. Her husband had done his 20 years as a soldier before becoming a civilian employee of the army, so she knew her way around the system. She also gained notoriety after a toilet bowl collapsed under her at a morning tea for army wives. Most accepted that there must have been a fault with the bowl, perhaps a crack or something. But less charitable people suggested that it may well have been the force of the reverberations that precipitated the collapse. Ollie took all the commotion in her stride.

She was a great ally for two motherless kids. If anything needed sorting out, she was never slow to draw up her considerable girth, don her infamous huge green coat and march off to do battle for them. Many a teacher had copped an earful from her. In fact, some would even disappear when they saw her coming.

Dad always joked that she wasn't the salt of the earth but more the pepper, because she knew how to get up people's noses and cause an adverse reaction. He reckoned that if she'd been a soldier, she would most definitely have been decorated for bravery. But underneath her gruff exterior, she was a lovely, kind-hearted old stick, and Tracy in particular missed her, although the two families still exchanged Christmas cards and looked forward eagerly to the army reunions.

Tracy was in a bad state. Her jaw ached badly and jutted out from the right side of her face like the Akaroa Peninsula. She was groggy from painkillers, antibiotics and lack of sleep, and dizzy from lack of food. It even hurt to swallow. Mac was right. She was not in a good frame of mind, but there were mitigating circumstances. She looked at her watch. Only 10.15am. Still more than 24 hours until her 11am appointment Wednesday. God, she hoped the bugger would pull it out tomorrow. No good shrugging her head in frustration, either, because that would only hurt. She'd got out of bed only once that morning, to go to the loo and let the dog in, and that had been bad enough. Mac had reasoned that Blade would be less likely to wander if he could come inside. He reckoned he might like company.

Hah, thought Tracy. Bloody company? Bullshit. The bloody thing hated her and she didn't trust it, either. That malicious grin and the sly way it slunk around behind you. It had caught her napping more than once. She rolled over and sunk the left side of her cheek gently into the pillow. Might as well try to get some sleep, she thought. Roll on tomorrow.

It was the growling that woke her up. Blade was in her room and growling. He never came in her room and very rarely growled. At first she thought she must have slept for hours and he needed to go outside. She glanced quickly at the alarm clock. Only 11.27am. "Okay, okay," she said to the dog and hauled herself painfully out of bed and staggered to the bedroom door. Blade scuttled off in front of her and stood by the back door, agitated and growling deeply.

Only now did she begin to realise that something was definitely up. With her aching jaw suddenly forgotten and her head rapidly clearing, she peered out through the kitchen curtain netting. There were three of them in the back yard, all young and roughly dressed. One big guy and two scrawny looking smaller ones. They didn't look like the sort of people who had a legitimate reason for being there, either.

Her heart gave a lurch and the wave of panic that threatened to engulf her was very similar to the time she'd been followed home from work. Hang on, hang on, don't panic, she thought. She opened the window a crack and yelled loudly: "What are guys you doing here? What do you want? If you don't bugger off, I'm calling the police!"

"It's only a fuckin' sheila," she heard one of them say. "We can still do it." The big bloke, the only one who didn't have a hoodie and sunglasses, agreed. "Yeah," he said, trying the back door. It was locked. "Hey bitch," he said, "we're coming in. Open the fuckin' door or I'll kick it in."

"I'm ringing the police!" she yelled. The booting on the door started as she turned to go back into the bedroom to get her mobile.

Jock hadn't seen the van come up the road because he'd been out the back. But he spotted it straight away when he walked around the front carrying his spade, and his trouble antenna immediately clicked into operation. It was out of place. He knew it shouldn't be there. Mac and Tracy surely would have said something. It wasn't good, with that girl was over there on her own.

Almost involuntarily he began crossing the road. The vehicle was the white, high-topped style favoured by couriers, with blacked-out back windows. As Jock approached, a young guy with those stupid fuckin' crutch pants and a hoodie over his head emerged from the driver's seat and stood by the open door, staring at the gate.

Jock immediately knew something was definitely up and used the bulk of the van to cover his approach. He was only two paces away when the young guy realised someone was there and turned quickly. "What are you doing here, laddie?" asked Jock. "What's it to you, old man?" came the sneering reply. Although he was a tough old rooster, Jock knew he knew he wasn't up to mixing it with a young guy for very long, especially when he didn't know how many others were lurking behind the fence.

He decided to skip the introductions. "This," was all he said as he swung the flat of the spade, catching the young punk on the left side of his face with a loud sponging noise. He went down and Jock was quickly on him, holding the sharp end of the spade across the dazed youngster's throat.

"You're up to no good, aren't you?" he asked. Then the banging and yelling could be heard from the yard. "Get up, get up, you young prick!" he yelled. "If they've hurt that girl, I'll have their balls." The young punk staggered gingerly to his feet and Jock prodded him roughly toward the gate.

Tracy could see the door was going to give way any minute, so she put her shoulder to it, giving up on getting the phone. She was oblivious to Blade dancing around eagerly behind her, just itching to get into the fray.

Another thump and the door sprang inwards. She jerked forward with her shoulder to try and slam it closed again, but there was a big boot in the way. Then an arm and a shoulder forced their way through the gap followed by a big ugly head. "It's a sheila in a nightie!" he called. "Looks like we might get some fucking in as well." An arm reached out grabbed her by the tit and squeezed hard.

Any fear in Tracy's mind suddenly disappeared as the blood ran into the eye and the brain clouded over. She stepped back from the door suddenly, which caught the thug by surprise. He lurched forward, narrowly avoiding falling. The eager Blade joined the action, ducking around the door and diving straight at the intruder's ankles. With a dog suddenly hanging on to his ankle for dear life, the guy stepped backward into the yard trying to shake him off. "Get off! Get off! You fuckin' mongrel!"

Tracy, with no real thought about it at all, grabbed Ollie and stepped out of the doorway. With the bat turned on its side, she made a vicious downward swipe, trying to smash the guy on the head. She missed his head but caught the ear, and then the bat smacked heavily into the collarbone with a satisfying thud.

The guy went down screaming, ear gushing blood. "You fuckin' bitch! I'll . . . " But Tracy wasn't finished. With an adrenaline-charged, fearsome crossbat swing, she smacked him fair in the side of the head with the face of the bat. Strike two. He went down and stayed there. Still with the rage on her Tracy clubbed him another three times before finally regaining control of her runaway emotions.

Meanwhile, Blade saw one of the others make a break for the gate and took off after him. Having seen the dog on his mate, this guy wanted nothing to do with him. In desperation, he jumped up and grabbed the top of the fence and tried to haul himself over. But he wasn't quick enough. Blade quickly latched on to an ankle and wasn't letting go for anything.

The guy struggled to pull himself up and over, but he had all that extra weight to lift and the pain, oh the fuckin' pain! He shrieked and dropped back to the ground, shaking the dog off in the process. But it was only a temporary reprieve and with the dog looming large again, he made another leap for the top of the fence. Blade also leapt and grabbed hold again, this time by the pants. Jock's much-hated, over-sized baggy-crutch pants. Fear lending him strength, the guy slithered hurriedly out of them and with considerable relief pulled himself up and over the fence, out of harm's way. Or so he thought. But there waiting for him on the other side was Jock with his spade.

Blade danced around below the fence excitedly. This was a great game. He was loving it. He saw Tracy standing above the big guy, spade in hand. Then he spotted the third guy, who had gone further on around the house trying the windows. He was just standing there motionless, as if mesmerised by all the action. But when he saw Blade eyeing him, he began to run.

Yippee! The dog was ecstatic and leapt into the attack. It was only a fair attempt to escape because Blade was on him before he got halfway to the gate. With one ankle in a dog's mouth, it is hard to run. The guy fell flat on his face, an exultant Blade all over him in a flash.

Jock had heard the guy on the fence shrieking and when he saw him on top of the fence, he prodded his prisoner heavily with the spade and growled: "Lie down, fuckhead." There was no argument. Then the fence-jumper fell heavily on to the driveway and lay sprawled out in a pair of rather grimy looking boxers. He was groaning with either pain or relief, or perhaps both.

With two captives to look after, things were getting a bit crowded. So just for good measure and to get his undivided attention, Jock clipped the fence-jumper on the side of the head with the flat of the spade, too. Not as hard as he had the first one, though. Just enough to make his eyeballs rattle a bit.

"Listen up, you two morons," he said. "When I tell you to stand up, stand up, and we're going to go through that gate. If you've hurt that girl in any way, I'll have ye balls! Ye ken?"

"I'm not going back in there," the second one cried. "That fuckin' dog's mad."

"Ye'll do what ye fuckin' told, laddie, or I'll bash ye with this again," said Jock, brandishing the spade. "Now get up, the both of ye!" The two got up and headed for the gate. "Open the fuckin' thing!" growled Jock. One of them obeyed. "Now get in there!"

Reluctantly but suitably encouraged by Jock's vigorous prodding, they entered the back yard. Jock was pleased to see the dog all over a guy lying in the middle of the lawn. He prodded his captives on to the lawn, well away from the gate, and brusquely told them to lie down. Both of them had eyes only for the dog and would have argued, but the wild look in Jock's eye was enough to make them obey.

"Lassie! Lassie!" he called. "Are ye all right?" Tracy got up from where, with adrenaline rush finally over, she had finally sagged exhaustedly against the porch wall. "Jock!" she cried. "I'm so pleased to see you." Tears began to roll. "These, these . . . tried to break in. I . . . " Unable to finish, she burst into tears.

"There, there, lassie, it's all over," said Jock. "They aren't going to be doing you any harm now." He looked down at the one Tracy had smashed with the cricket bat. "Jayze," he said. "You've give this one a good wee nudge. I'd say he's probably concussed, by the look of it."

With the blood running from the ear and a swollen head covered with abrasions, the unconscious thug presented a fearsome sight. Tracy shuddered. "Oh my god, you don't think I've killed him do you? The bastard grabbed me by the . . . " Unable to say the word, she indicated her breast. "He hurt me."

Jock had a quick look at the unconscious thug, felt his pulse, then said: "Nay he'll live. Listen, lassie, don't be having any regrets. They came looking for trouble and found it. All ye've done is defend yourself, and you're entitled to do that."

A loud scream pierced the air. They both looked over to see Blade having the time of his life. He had somehow got his victim's crutch pants down far enough to rip his undies, and now he had a mouthful of arse.

"Do you have a leash for that dog?" Jock laughed. "We better pull him off yon moron before the cops get here."

"Yes, we do," said Tracy. "You don't think Blade will get in the shit, do you?"

"Nae, nae," said Jock. "It'd be poor show if they blamed the dog. If it wasn't for him, who knows what might have happened?"

Between the two of them, they managed to slip the leash on Blade and, with some difficulty, dragged him away to tie him up by the gate.

"Jayze, look at the state of that one's undies too," Jock said. "Do their mothers not teach them how to wipe their arses properly these days?" Despite herself, Tracy had to laugh.

"Ye better go and ring the police now," Jock said, then looked at the one Tracy had bashed. "Tell them to send an ambulance too. Tell them it was an attempted home invasion. That'll get their attention."

He moved off toward the prone would-be thieves brandishing his spade while Tracy went in to get the phone. With experience in the security industry after his discharge from the army, Jock was well aware of the law regarding citizen's arrest and depriving someone of their liberty.

He said to the three conscious hoods: "I'm not detaining ye. Ye can leave whenever you like. Of course, I don't know what the dog will think about that. Do ye?" They all looked fearfully at Blade tied very strategically on a long lead by the gate. Nobody moved.

While waiting for the police and ambulance, Jock had a quiet word to Tracy about what was likely to occur. "The defence lawyers will probably try and make out that they are little angels who were just misunderstood and that we have committed a grave assault on them," he said.

"So you just stick to your guns and say that you were at home alone sick in bed when they kicked the door in, indecently assaulted you and threatened you with rape. Don't be afraid to gild the lily because for sure their lawyers will try and do that for them. Do ye understand what I'm saying, lassie?"

"I think so, Jock," she said. "Good. Now best put that bat back inside, then we'll tie the dog up at his kennel. But I'll keep the spade handy, just in case."

It was a full house at Mac and Tracy's the following Saturday. "You look so much better since you've had that tooth out," Millie told Tracy as they prepared food in the kitchen. "It feels a lot better too, thank God," said Tracy. "You know, I was thinking if I hadn't been home, I wonder what would have happened?"

"Don't worry" said Millie. "You did well. Silly old Jock and Blade would have probably sorted it out, anyway." The two picked up the plates of food and went into the lounge, greeted by a cheer from Mac as he nursed a beer with Blade lolling at his feet.

At the dining table, Jock and Tracy's Dad were addressing a whisky bottle, Scotch of course, and having a good catch up.

"Oh, Dad," said Tracy. "I had a ring from Terry. He said that the mother of one of those idiots rang the council and put in a complaint about Blade. She reckoned they all had to have tetanus injections and take antibiotics for the injuries he inflicted, and she wants him put down."

"It's the poor wee dog that needs the shots. given the state of the underpants I saw," interjected Jock. That bought a laugh. Jock continued: "Aye, I see there's been some debate over the level of violence we used, too. That one ye bashed is still in hospital . . ." Tracy tried to interject. "But, but . ." Jock held up his hand. "Don't you be worrying, lassie. That thug grabbed you. He said he was going to rape you. You had every right to do what you did, and it would be a poor sort of a court that didn't agree."

Her Dad broke in. "Jock's right, Tracy. I am very proud of you. That woman's got a bloody cheek, all right. If her idiot son pleads not guilty and it does go to trial and you're getting a hard time off his smart-arse lawyer, all you have to say is: And what would you have me do, sir, let him have his way? That'll stir 'em up."

Mac chipped in "He'll probably say you should have negotiated your way out of it." That crack bought general laughter and snorts of derision from Jock, who said: "Aye, with the barrel of a gun."

Millie broke in. "Hush, you men. Stop putting ideas in the poor girl's head. It'll probably never come to that, anyway. Have something to eat. You must be worn out from the blarney you've have been talking all morning." Laughter again and then Tracy's father asked: "By the way, who's Terry anyway?"

"Oh, he's one of the policeman that came. He was very nice and helpful. Actually, he's coming around to see how I am later."

"Terry, is it?" said her father with a big smile. "Not constable or officer, then." Tracy reddened but chose to ignore the bait and continued: "Anyway, as I was saying, the council rang the police to find out what happened but Terry said his sergeant put them straight. Told them Blade was a hero who helped break up a well-organised gang of thieves. Oh, by the way, one of them admitted to five other burglaries and gave police the name of the second-hand dealer they were selling the stolen items to, and they've done a raid already. So it's all good."

"Excellent. Looks like Blade's off the hook, then," said her Dad. "Actually, Mac, I reckon if you nail some battens on the top of the fence and then run shade cloth along it, that might stop the bugger getting out. Whadya reckon?"

"Worth a try" said Mac. "I'll do it tomorrow. But he's a pretty ingenious sort of a bugger. He'll probably find another way out."

"I haven't finished yet" butted in Tracy. "Well, what then?" said Mac. "Terry said that his sergeant said to say well done to all of us and to give the dog a bone."

They all burst into laughter and Jock said: "Aye, we'll do that, we'll do just that, lassie. The wee bugger's certainly earned it."

TO BE SURE,
TO BE SURE

Peedee was a real mongrel. That sounds awful, I know, but the fact is that he was a dog. Probably about half bull terrier, but with several other unknown bits and pieces thrown into the mix. He was a dark brindle in colour, with black piercing eyes that made him look sinister and threatening to those who didn't know him. But in reality he was, if you'll excuse the expression, a real pussy, an out-and-out kids' dog.

Oh, he'd bark loudly, sound and look ferocious if a stranger came up the drive or to the back gate. But if they only took a moment to let him sniff their hand, he'd invariably regard them as a friend and let them in. Most people didn't hang around long enough to discover this fact, however. If no one was at home to answer the door, they'd generally bolt from this mean-looking critter. He was prized for his ability to keep Bible-bangers and salesmen from the door.

Peedee belonged to my nephew Paul. He and a previous girlfriend had seen him at the RSPCA one day and fallen instantly in love. It hadn't taken too much persuasion for them to walk out of there a few hundred dollars lighter in pocket but the proud owners of a lively and curious brindle ball of energy that had been jabbed, stabbed and inoculated. He showed his intelligence and character right from day one, too. Paul had to do a hasty fencing job on their back yard so he didn't wander while they were at work and university, and for some months they thought this had done the trick.

But one Saturday morning, as they passed the local garage while walking down to the beach, they were surprised when one of the mechanics called out: "Hullo, Peedee."

A short conversation revealed that he had been getting out every morning for some weeks and wandering over there to spend most of the day with the grease-monkeys, generally leaving around 3pm to be at home when his owners got back. Of course he had been the recipient of the odd snack and a scratch as well, and with his name on his collar, he'd soon become a regular member of the team.

My nephew had cracked up at that. "You cunning little shit," he'd said at the time. He didn't even bother to find the hole in the fence. Ingenuity like that deserved its reward, he reckoned.

Sadly, Paul's relationship with that girlfriend ended about a year later and he found himself having to move into a box-like apartment near the uni with absolutely no place for dogs. What do they say? One person's misfortune is another person's gain. When Paul asked me if Peedee could live with us, my 15-year-old Down Syndrome boy was over the moon. He'd played with Peedee several times and they'd taken to each other like ducks to water. And I do mean like ducks to water. We had a swimming pool and the two would muck around in there for hours, Peedee absolutely adoring the water. In fact he'd always start yelping when my nephew turned his old bomb into our street, because he just knew he was going for a swim with my son. Peedee and my son both came to excel in diving and retrieving stuff from the bottom of the pool, even at the deep end. I never did quite discover who taught who.

It was about this time I began working with an Irishman from Dublin with the splendid name of Seamus O'Murtagh. We had started at the company at the same time and went through the same induction. We both had a military background and a common penchant for taking the piss. We had immediately got on well together. He had the great sense of humour that the Irish tend to have and I remember that when we started work at this company, a very self-opinionated Englishman immediately came on to Seamus, as though to prove the Irish were inferior to the English.

The first time I heard him, I said to Seamus: "You don't wanna be taking that shit from that ignorant Pommy bastard. You want me to fix him up?"

"Away wit' ya, Mick," Seamus said. "You'll only get yoursel' in the shite. Leave it wit' me, I'll fix him up."

And fix him he did, but definitely not in the way I'd expected. Seamus bided his time until one day when we were all assembled for one of the meetings with management that was called from time to time.

"Hey, Cedric," Seamus called out to the Pom. "They reckoned that you're not fit to wipe management's arse. But I stuck up for you. I said you were."

Everyone cracked up, and even more so when a somewhat confused Cedric replied: "Thanks, Seamus." He wasn't that smart at all, that particular English gentleman.

Seamus and I began to have the odd beer together and then he came over for a barbecue one Sunday, bringing his wife Bridie. My son and Peedee put on a diving exhibition for them and they were both amazed at what that dog could do under water.

Like most people, Bridie was a bit wary of Peedee at first. But after being around him for a while and seeing what a pussy he was, she began to loosen up. Both she and Seamus had delightfully thick Irish brogues, with Bridie in particular being hard to understand – especially when excited. She was an interesting and rather confusing blend of common sense, superstition, Celtic mysticism and downright devout religiousness when she saw fit.

I sometimes went round to their place on a weekend for a meal as well, and I'd always take a bottle of wine for her. As a rule she wouldn't start drinking until after 8pm, and Seamus always used to joke that the bottle was always gone by half past. Bridie vehemently denied this, of course. One time when I was at their place we were out on the patio having a beer. Well, Seamus and I were. Bridie hadn't started drinking. Too early for her, although the bottle of wine I'd bought over had been eagerly squirrelled away for later.

When Seamus went in to check on the dinner, Bridie said to me: "You know, when we were first married, Shammy hardly gave me a chance to take me cardy off." Not quite sure where this conversation was going, I just nodded. Then with a faraway look in her eye, she continued: "Now, I've time to knit one." I looked to see if she was having me on or not, but her face had this serious wistful look on it. So I just shook quietly with laughter.

Another time, I went around for a meal when she'd been off colour for a while and had been undergoing tests for various ailments, including cancer. Knowing she'd not been feeling well, I thought I'd take flowers instead of wine. When I went in, she was lying on the couch looking rather weak and pale. She regarded the flowers with a baleful eye then looked me up and down before declaring: "I ain't fecken dead yet, ye know." Thus chastised, I went down the road and bought the obviously expected bottle of wine.

About this time, one of my nieces was getting married. My nephew Paul was one of the groomsmen and the whole family was invited. It had been in the planning for well over a year now. It would be the first gathering of the clan since my Mum passed away two years previously and it would have pleased her tremendously.

Because the venue was several hundred kilometres away, where my niece and her partner both worked, we all decided we'd stay on for a week or even longer. Accommodation was organised and paid for, lots of activities planned and everyone was looking forward to the wedding and family reunion.

Peedee had now been with us for over two years and was well ensconced as another and important member of the family, more especially to my son, who was very excited about the upcoming wedding and family gathering. I had imagined Peedee would stay at our house while we were away, and Seamus had offered to feed and take him for a walk daily.

But here I was wrong. My nephew had a new girlfriend, a lovely girl called Mary, who was also a Peedee fan. She was concerned about him having to stay on his own for a week and suggested that instead he be left at her brother's place, about 80km away in a semi-rural setting with plenty of roaming space plus company for the dog.

Most thought that was a good idea except Seamus and Bridie, who had been looking forward to looking after him. I did feel a bit guilty about this but as the dog was still technically my nephew's, I went along with the decision and explained this to Seamus, who was okay with it then.

So away we went to the wedding, thinking all was well. It was actually during the reception when the call came on my nephew's cellphone: Peedee had disappeared. He hadn't been there the previous evening when Mary's brother and his family arrived home and despite an intensive search throughout the day, there had been no sign of him.

Mary was distraught and close to tears, blaming herself because it had been her suggestion to leave him there. She wanted to return home straight away to help look for him. Paul and I both assured her that Peedee was smart and he'd turn up and anyway. If we went back, what could we do that hadn't been done already?

My brother also rightfully commented that it was his daughter's day and we didn't want to spoil it. He was also pretty sure the dog would turn up eventually. Somewhat mollified, Mary perked up and we returned our minds back to the proceedings.

The week's holiday drifted quickly by and there was still no word of the dog. My nephew became increasingly morose and my son was also upset. It threw a real pall on what was supposed to be a happy occasion and I think we were all relieved when it eventually came time to board the plane for home.

Peedee had been missing for 10 days now. My son, who didn't quite understand just where he'd gone missing, walked around the neighbourhood calling his name. Mary was in tears quite often now, and Paul had a face on him like thunder most of the time. Seamus and Bridie came over to sympathise and had the good grace not to say what they could have. It wasn't a particularly nice time for any of us at all.

Two days later, still no dog. I was sitting out on the patio after work, nursing a beer and thinking. 'Come on Peedee, where are you boy?" In walked Bridie. "Mitill," she said in her impossibly broad accent. "What ye have tae do is go down to da church, pray to Saint Auntinee, put $5 in da poor box and da dog'll come back."

Yeah right, I thought. Being an old soldier, I'm a bit of a sceptic when it comes to religion. Most of the trouble in the world today seems to be caused by one religion or another thinking they're the only ones who've got it right.

"Will ye do it then?" she persisted. "I'm not going into a church to pray for a bloody dog," I said. "I don't even pray for myself."

"Ye have tae do it if ye want da dog back," she said.

I had a swig of my beer, shaking my head contemptuously, and she went off muttering to herself. Something about bleddy heathens, if I heard correctly. Despite myself, I had a bit of a laugh.

"Superstitious thing. As if that's going to bring the dog back," I said to no one.

The next day, Friday, Bridie bowled in again. "I'm going ta Mass ta-morrah. I'm going ta pray ta Aaint Auntinee for da dog and I'm not leaving here till ya gi' me $5."

Giving up, I dug into my pocket and threw a $10 note at her. "Here," I said, "might as well ask Him for the Lotto numbers while you're there, then."

She went off at me: "Ya don't blaspheme or ask for money or he won't do anyting for ya!" she said. "Yer a bleddy Heathen!" Thoroughly disgusted at my lack of faith, she left, shaking her head in disapproval.

That night, Seamus and I went to the pub for a couple of hours then had a few whiskeys at my place. A good old Irish wake, solemnly saluting the passing of the dog. "Da foinest dog dis side of the Liffey," Seamus proclaimed. As the tide went out in the bottle and the alcohol rose in our systems, he cracked up when I did my terrible imitation of Bridie: "Ya pray tae Saint Auntinee, ya put $5 in da poor box and da dog'll come back."

"I wouldn't let her hear you saying that," Seamus said between laughs, tears rolling down his cheeks.

"It's been over two weeks now, Seamus," I told him. "He's either dead or someone's got him. They fight dogs like him, you know." He shook his head sadly. "I tink you're right dere. Slainte." We toasted the dog.

Next morning, as was my usual habit of a Sunday and although I had a wee bit of a head on me, I got up early, quietly got ready then went out and got my mountain bike out of the shed. I tried to do at least two hours of bike riding every Sunday. Sometimes I was a bit scratchy for half an hour or so but I eventually came right if I persisted, something I'd learned long ago in the army.

I wheeled my bike out to the front of the house, put it on the stand and had just begun to do a few light stretches when a slight movement behind me caught my peripheral vision. I turned, and there on the mat was sprawled a brindle bundle.

"Peedee!" I called. His tail wagged, his eyes glistened and his tongue lolled but he didn't move. I walked over and soon saw why. He'd been travelling hard. He had lost a lot of weight and was very gaunt. His paws were torn and bleeding, with claws worn right down to the pads, and the skin was ripped on one hip. It looked like he'd been hit by a car. But he was alive and he was home safely! Reluctantly, he limped round the back with me and slumped thankfully on to his mat. I woke my son up with the news and he was over the moon, making a big fuss of the dog. I let him give Peedee a small meal and some water. It looked like he hadn't eaten for a while and we didn't want him to be sick, as I pointed out before I got on the phone to spread the news.

First my brother arrived, then Paul and Mary. With tears in her eyes, she sat on the old couch in the patio hugging the dog, saying: "Peedee, Peedee, where have you been?"

As if he understood the question, he began to howl: "Ow-ow-ow-ow-ow-ow." He went on like this for about a minute before finally lapsing into silence.

"What did he say, Dad?" my son asked. "He said you took me to somewhere I didn't know and left me there," I answered. "And all I wanted to do was come home but I didn't realise how far it was, and now look at me." They all laughed when my son asked quite seriously: "Did he really say that, Dad?"

Later, after Mary and Paul had taken the dog to the vet for a check-up, I suddenly thought: "God, I'll have to tell Seamus and Bridie. I'll never hear the end of it."

I was right. When they came over later in the afternoon, Bridie was exultant. "Ya see, ya see, ya heathen beggar. Ya would na' listen tae me. Ya pray ta Saint Auntinee, ya put money in da poor box and ya get what ya lost back."

I was just about to concede that she had been right when she continued: "Now, ya have ta tank him by putting more money in da poor box, or he'll take someting offa ya."

I was through arguing with her. You couldn't fight that sort of logic, or was it illogic? I silently handed over another tenner.

She wasn't through, though. "And next time ya going away, ya better let us look after da dog."

"Why's that, Dad?" my son innocently asked. Seamus immediately jumped in with a big smile on his face. "For da same reason an Irishman allus wears two condoms," he said. "To be sure to be sure."

We all burst out laughing while my son and Peedee looked at us as if we were all completely mad. Perhaps we were.

JUST DESSERTS

Cyril McGonagle was a short, stocky, sandy-haired boy who was usually very happy and contented, with a huge affectionate smile for everyone. And so it should have been on this particular Friday morning. He was up early as usual, having had his 10 hours' uninterrupted sleep. How he consistently slept so well and for so long, even under adverse circumstances, was a source of wonder and amazement to his parents and siblings. He'd made his own bed and got his own breakfast, although not before feeding his best pal, a real bitser of a dog called PD, which was short for Pound Dog because that's where he'd originally come from. Cyril's Dad always claimed he should really have been called Pool Dog, because he seemed to spend half his life swimming and diving in the family's pool.

Cyril did the dishes after breakfast, put them all away and generally tidied up as quietly as possible. He didn't want to wake Mum because she didn't knock off work until 3am and was generally sound asleep by the time he got up. Yep, Fridays were usually a good day for him. It was the last day of school before the weekend and he got to buy his lunch instead of having to make it. To top it all off, he also got pocket money for keeping the house tidy during the week. Mum usually left the money on the bench for him before she went to bed, and that was the first thing he looked for when he got up on Fridays.

He always liked it a lot better when Dad was at home in the mornings, though. They always mucked about and had a few laughs together. But Dad was a casual worker; his roster always varied and he never really knew what the next week was going to bring.

Dad always said that when you were only a casual worker, you were at the mercy of the person who drew up the rosters, and generally got only the shifts that no one else wanted. But if you didn't take what they offered you, or work hard and keep your mouth shut, you mightn't be invited back. So you just had to grin and bear it.

He also reckoned the casuals and the more motivated permanent workers had to carry the lazier workers on their backs, and it just wasn't fair. They had to work that much harder to cover for the bludgers. But there didn't seem to be any real way of getting rid of them either, he'd said, apart from asess-assasing them – that was the funny-sounding word Dad had used. When Cyril had asked Mum what it meant, she said it meant killing people but that Dad had only been joking.

Mum and Dad could both be a bit grumpy at times, especially when they were overtired, but that was understandable, what with the odd hours they worked. Cyril somehow understood and was always happy to see them anyway. But on this particular Friday, Cyril was reluctant to leave for school. It wasn't that he didn't like school, or his teachers and friends, and doing his lessons and playing cricket at lunchtimes. No, it wasn't that at all. In fact, he loved all that stuff and usually missed it terribly when they had school holidays.

The problem was those boys from that other school who caught the same bus as him in the mornings. Four or five of them, there were, aged about 14 or 15. They got on at the next two or three stops after his, and lately they had begun teasing and laughing at him, and calling him names that he didn't like much.

Earlier in the week, one of them had even threatened to beat him up because he'd just kept ignoring them while they teased him. He was very relieved when the bus finally reached the stop where he got off. The harassment had been going on for more than a month now, turning his once pleasant and looked-forward-to morning bus trip into total misery. He had come to dread it.

Dad had always told him not to take any notice if anyone called him names or teased him. Just ignore them, he'd said. And up until now, Cyril had done just that. But these boys were becoming bolder and bolder each morning, and getting that much harder to ignore.

The only good thing was that they never seemed to be on the bus home, so at least that was still okay.

He didn't really want to tell Dad about it, either, Not after what happened a few years ago when three boys attacked him when he was coming home from school one day. Dad had gone right off his face and, when he found out who they were, charged straight up to the house of the ringleader's parents.

Finding the boy at home but his parents out, Dad had apparently manhandled him rather roughly, shaking him severely. After strongly warning him never to do it again, he'd gone straight round to the other boys' homes as well. Luckily for both of them, at least one of their parents had been home at the time. Dad told them what had happened and had said that if it wasn't safe for his boy to come home from school unmolested, then it wouldn't be safe for theirs either. When one of the fathers had asked him if that was a threat, Dad had said no, it wasn't a threat. But it was definitely a promise.

Later that afternoon, the ringleader's Mum arrived home, found her boy in tears and found out what had happened. She rang the police, who'd come to see Dad and told him he'd probably be charged with assault. Dad was unrepentant and determined. Fair enough, he'd told the cops. They could charge him with assault. But the boy's parents should know that he'd make sure the papers knew who they were and what they'd done.

Funnily enough, no charges ever eventuated. The father of the ringleader had even come round the following day, shaking hands with both Dad and Cyril, apologising, saying there was no hard feelings and that he would have probably done the same thing himself.

Dad reckoned the only reason the parents hadn't pressed charges was because they didn't want their little darling's name, and the school he went to, plastered across the paper. Mum had been awfully embarrassed about the whole thing, saying that she wouldn't ever be able to look those parents in the eye again. But Dad had said no, that it was they who shouldn't be able to look her in the eye.

So Cyril didn't want to tell Dad about his current predicament. He didn't want him going off half-cocked again and perhaps getting into trouble for it. He didn't much like it when Dad got mad. It upset him. And Mum said when he did lose it, sometimes he went a bit too far. On the odd occasion Dad got it all wrong anyway, and went mad about nothing. After the last episode, Mum had told him that if anything like that ever happened again, he was to tell only her and not Dad. But he didn't really like to bother her with his troubles. She always seemed so tired.

So what to do? The boys on the morning bus were getting worse and worse. One of them had even pushed him as he'd got off yesterday. Cyril wasn't an aggressive boy and he wasn't the quickest thinker in the world, either. He was a very gentle, good-natured and placid boy who just couldn't understand why the others were picking on him. All he knew was that he didn't like being pushed, laughed at, called a four-eyed wanker, a four-eyed freak and some of the other names they called him, some of them including the F word. It was really beginning to upset him.

Very reluctantly, he headed off to the bus stop, pausing to make sure he locked the front door properly and double-checking it too, as he had been so patiently taught by his mum. At 16 years old, Cyril wasn't really equipped to deal with the trouble he was facing – not that he should have had to, anyway. Dad always claimed Cyril was no ordinary boy. He might have been born with Down Syndrome, but he was pretty smart.

The family was shocked at first when Cyril was born with Down Syndrome. But their doctor was terrific and talked them through how it occurred. He also explained how, in a lot of ways, people with Down Syndrome were far better off than others. They never worry or stress about anything, he'd said. If they lived a long life, which was quite on the cards in Cyril's case, their faces would remain without all the wrinkles that everyday living and stress produce in the rest of us.

To a certain extent his family had found this to be true. Cyril had proved to be pretty good at forgetting things, and especially nasty things. When he was sick, he didn't cry or carry on like normal kids. He'd usually just go straight to sleep – any time, day or night – and sleep for hours. Yes, his sleeping habits confounded the rest of his family. When he was tired, he'd just announce he was going to bed. Five minutes later, he'd be sound asleep, and remain so for the rest of the night

Everyone else wished they could do that, especially his Mum and Dad working split shifts. Their bodies never quite knew whether they were supposed to be awake or asleep. His older brother Matt was openly envious and asked Cyril how he did it. Cyril couldn't really say. He reckoned it just happened when he closed his eyes. "You egg," was Matt's exasperated reply.

Thinking about it, which he did quite often, Cyril's Dad became more and more convinced that the older children were a major reason the boy was doing so well. There had been no shortage of advice when Cyril was born. Some well-meaning and misguided people even told them Down Syndrome kids were dumb, needed to be protected and should be institutionalised, as they routinely were in earlier times. But his parents took their doctor's words on board. They vowed to bring Cyril up exactly as his brother and sister were being brought up, with very little allowance for his being a Down Syndrome boy. He was taught to do the same things as the others: Make his own bed, wash the dishes, help around the house, whatever – even if it did take him a bit longer to learn.

With both Dad and Mum working nights, Cyril had been left with his brother and sister quite a lot, and they'd taught him quite a few things he wasn't supposed to be able to do. For instance, Mum and Dad had been told Cyril would probably never have sufficient balance or co-ordination to master riding a two-wheeler bike. But someone must have forgotten to tell Matt.

After Cyril had finally grown out of his three-wheeler, Matt had simply put him up on his own bike and pushed him off down their slightly sloped section. Initially, he'd either fall off on the lawn or, if he did manage to stay upright long enough, crash headlong into the hedge, much to Dad's chagrin. But Cyril thought it was great fun and eventually, after a few years of this rough-and-tumble enjoyment, he'd actually developed enough balance and co-ordination to be able to keep himself upright. Well, most of the time anyway.

When he was finally deemed competent enough to actually ride on the road, he had a bit of trouble choosing which side of the road to ride on. Picking left from right proved to be a bit of a problem, but eventually he got it all sorted. Cyril had also developed extremely good hand-eye co-ordination, courtesy of the endless cricket games played in the back yard with both his brother and sister, with even Mum and Dad joining in sometimes. He was a rather good batsman and not too bad a bowler, either.

He could also play an excellent game of pool, having had plenty of practice on the table in the family's garage. Matt always laughed when he remembered the time the family over the road bought a pool table and their two sons invited him and Cyril over for a game. Cyril had easily cleaned them both up, much to their embarrassment and their father's delight. They were full of excuses, of course, but they improved greatly with practice. Still, Cyril continued giving them a good run for their money.

Actually, Peter from over the road was a great mate to Cyril and they quite often went bike riding or walked PD together. One day they let him off the lead (against strict instructions) well before they got to the park. One of PD's few faults had proved to be an instinctive hatred of cats. While he was generally obedient and playful, all bets were off if he saw a cat and wasn't restrained quickly enough.

So on this day, PD saw a cat in a garden. He charged at it and a big fight ensued. PD was getting far the better of the cat when Cyril turned to Peter and asked innocently: "Are they playing?"

"No, he's killing that cat!" the horrified Peter yelled. "Get him!" Somehow, the two boys managed to haul the dog off and beat a hasty retreat. They brought him home, not saying a word about the fight. They thought they'd gotten away with it until, some hours later, there was a knock at the door.

Dad opened it and there was a woman standing there who immediately burst out: "Your dog nearly killed my cat, it can't even walk."

When Dad finally got to the bottom of the story, he apologised profusely to the woman, saying: "Look, I'm sure the boys didn't intend this to happen. Dogs have probably been chasing cats since Adam and Eve. They probably consider it their job. Take your cat to the vet, bring the bill to me and I'll take care of it. In the meantime, I'll have a little word to them about letting the dog off the lead around houses."

Somewhat placated, the woman departed and, funnily enough, they never heard from her again. Both the boys always wondered if the cat had lived or died, but they were never game enough to go and ask.

Cyril was eventually taught to read and write, thanks to the combined efforts of the school, his mother, brother and sister. It took a fair bit of effort because his concentration wandered easily, but again constant repetition eventually prevailed.

Cyril also loved answering the phone. One day, when Dad was expecting a message from work but had to go down to the shopping centre for a few minutes, he asked Cyril to answer the phone for him if it should ring. Either write down the message or tell the caller to ring back in 10 minutes, Dad had told him.

Cyril happily agreed and as Dad had walked out the door, he'd asked him what was for dinner. "Mince pie," said Dad, which made Cyril really happy because, topped with tomato sauce, it was one of his all-time favourites. Dad got back less than 10 minutes later and asked Cyril if the phone had rung. "Yep,' said Cyril, "and I wrote the message down." When Dad looked at the pad he couldn't stop himself laughing at what was written: "My Dad has gone and he will be back in 10 a mince pie."

Another one of Cyril's adventures was also a classic that they all remembered well. Both his older siblings delivered pamphlets for a bit of pocket money. Cyril used to accompany them, graduating his own round when he got a bit older. This, of course, was after he finally learned that you couldn't put 20 of the same pamphlets into one letterbox to get rid of them that much quicker. With his happy, smiling face, he soon got to know many of the people in the neighbourhood, particularly the elderly, and he had begun to take the pamphlets in to some of them, sometimes to be rewarded with lollies, biscuits or chocolate.

One Sunday there was a knock at the door and when Dad opened it, there was an elderly lady standing there. "Are you Cyril's father?" she asked. "I must tell you this, it's absolutely delightful. Cyril has been bringing the pamphlets in for me and I sometimes give him sweets or biscuits in return.

"This morning when he bought them in, I said, 'Thank you, Cyril, that's very good of you'. He replied, 'That's all right, have you got any more of those chocolate biscuits?' When I said, 'No', he said, 'Why not?' I said, 'Because I haven't been shopping yet,' and he said, 'Do you want me to wait here while you go shopping?'"

Both Dad and the lady both burst out laughing and when Dad tried to apologise, the lady wouldn't have it. She said it was beautiful, the best laugh she'd had this year, and Dad was not to tell him off.

Cyril had given his family many funny and magic moments like these. He was pretty special and they loved him. But now Cyril was out of his depth trying to cope with the bullying on the bus. Most kids probably would be. It was a real worry to Cyril and he just didn't know what to do about it.

A couple of suburbs away lived old Bert, a wiry and gnarled old ex-soldier who was rapidly approaching the grand old age of 85. Bert was still as sprightly as ever, however, and had a part-time job as a cleaner at a pub. He'd known the publican, Jim, for years and was paid cash in hand, which was a real help in making ends meet on the pension. Bert was a slow worker but very thorough, and did an excellent job. Jim reckoned he was far better and much more reliable than a lot of the younger people he'd tried previously.

Bert was a trifle deaf, too, the old ears having suffered damage during his military service. Consequently, he shouted when he spoke. People always had to yell back at him to be heard in return, making him a rather well-known character in the pub. He usually had the odd beer before he went home. Most of his friends and acquaintances admired Bert's get-up-and-go, especially at his age. They thought the world of him.

He had been an early bird all his working life. He liked starting early, and it was hard breaking the habit of a lifetime. Jim always liked to joke that he'd be early for his own funeral if he could. "It's too bloody late for that now," old Bert would usually retort.

So this Friday was no exception and he was early to the bus stop to get to work. He wasn't too impressed with the three boys waiting with him. Their language was absolutely appalling. Despite his deafness, he could hear the swearwords they used constantly, seeming not to care that women were present. The arrogant young fools were blocking the footpath, too, so passers-by had to step on to the road to get around them. Bert shook his head and clicked his tongue in annoyance, ruing the fact that there was no corporal punishment in the schools any more. The old strap had never done him any harm, he reckoned.

The bus eventually pulled in and as he waited for his turn to board, the three boys pushed in ahead to make sure of getting seats. Bert clicked his tongue again. No manners at all. What on earth did they teach them in the schools these days? He boarded, showed the bus driver his pass, sat down right up the front and let his mind drift into memories. The bus continued its run and as more kids got on,

Bert slowly became aware of some sort of chanting coming from the back.

At first he paid it no mind. But at one bus stop, it got louder and louder as the bus moved off, and eventually he turned around for a look. It was those boys from his bus stop again. They'd been joined by a couple of others, by the look of it, and were pointing at another boy, laughing and calling him names. Good on the other bloke though, Bert thought. He wasn't taking the slightest bit of notice of them, though this seemed to whip the mob into more of a frenzy.

Bert looked again. The boy they were picking on looked familiar. Bert squinted, trying to see if he could make out who it was, but his 85-year-old eyes wouldn't play the game. His reading glasses wouldn't be of too much help from that distance, either.

One of Bert's greatest vanities was his claim that he needed glasses only for reading. This was more than a trifle optimistic, but he'd never be caught dead wearing glasses for anything other than that. It didn't matter, anyway, because just then the bus driver yelled at the boys to keep it down and the noise dropped slightly. Bert went back to his musings. But as the bus travelled along, he became aware that the chanting from the back was growing louder once more.

As the bus pulled into the next stop, it became outright yelling. He turned to look and saw two of the rude boys from his stop suddenly push the other one, whom they'd been calling names, as he went to get off at the rear entrance.

The boy stumbled down the step. But luckily, he had a firm enough grip on the handrail and managed to right himself without toppling over, and stepped out the now-open door. The rest of the bullies laughed idiotically and Bert felt a tinge of annoyance. Surely the bus driver should do something about that, he thought. But the driver was busy with the boarding passengers and had completely missed the side play.

Bert looked as the boy walked past his window. He seemed okay. He looked again, realising he did know that boy. That's old what's-his-name's son, he thought. He comes down to the pub with his father sometimes on a Sunday afternoon. Loves playing pool, and not too bad at it, either. He was one of those Special Olympics kids – Bert struggled to remember the right term. Down Syndrome, that was it. There were different names back in his heyday. He became more angry about what he'd just witnessed. The miserable so-and-sos, picking on a kid like that. I'll have a word with his father, that's what I'll do. He'll want to do something about this.

He made a mental note: I must remember to do that. The old memory plays tricks on me sometimes, but this is important. The poor kid shouldn't have to put up with that sort of carry-on. I'll tell Jim when I get to work, that's what I'll do. One of us should remember to tell old what's-his name when he comes down the pub next time. Satisfied with his decision, old Bert settled back into his reverie.

Cyril didn't go down to the pub with his father the following Sunday. His older brother Matt had come to visit and they were having fun in the pool with PD, the totally mad swimming and diving dog. Cyril had started it all off when they were playing in the shallow end one day, somehow teaching PD to retrieve stuff from the bottom of the pool. This ability had gradually developed until now he could even retrieve stuff from the deep end, which was quite amazing really.

He looked a bit like a seal, diving in head-first with front legs tucked in and using his weight to plane down and pick up the object off the bottom. But you had to watch him closely if you were in the pool yourself, as he was liable to jump right on top of you and his claws could scratch you quite badly. Of course, he was only playing. But after copping a couple of PD's bombs and suffering long scratches, Dad had declared him a regular shipping hazard in the water.

Meanwhile down at the pub, old Bert needed to be prompted by Jim before he remembered to tell Cyril's Dad about the incident. Cyril's Dad thanked him profusely and brought him a beer. Then he sat by himself for a while, deep in thought.

He knew he had been really lucky not to have been charged last time, so he'd better take it easy this time and not lose his cool. He also knew his wife had told Cyril not to report any further bullying to him, but to tell her only. Cyril had told him that. Really, his wife should have known better. Cyril was the world's worst secret-keeper. Still, he'd have to play it carefully, Dad thought. He knew it upset Cyril when he lost his temper, and he didn't really want to do that anyway.

I'll ring the other boys' school, he finally decided. That's the way to go. That's what I'll do. I'll give them the chance to sort it out. He rejoined his mates at their table.

The following Monday, Cyril's Dad had no luck getting hold of the principal of the offending boys' school. He always either seemed to be in a meeting, on the phone or with someone. He left his phone number with the secretary, but that didn't produce a result.

But Tuesday was his last day off before returning to work and when he found out that Cyril had been bullied again the day before, he was keen to get some sort of complaint registered. He settled for the deputy principal. But she didn't want to believe him.

"Our students just wouldn't do that, Mr McGonagle," she said. "This school prides itself on our student achievement and behaviour. Are you quite sure the boys are from this school?"

"My son may have Down Syndrome but he can read names on blazers," came the answer. "And then there is also the witness who informed me of their behaviour. So yes, they are from your school and they are bullying my son.

"Now, I'm prepared to give you the opportunity to sort it out," he continued. "But be aware that if it doesn't cease forthwith, and it's not safe for my boy to get to school unmolested, then unfortunately, you might find that it might not be safe for those boys either."

"That sounds very much like a threat to me, sir," the deputy head replied in a severe and now raised voice.

"No, not a threat at all," came the reply. "It's definitely a promise. Now, may I leave the matter in your hands?"

"We'll look into it, sir," said the deputy. "But I still find it hard to believe it's our pupils doing this. You must be mistaken."

"There's no mistake, madam," said Cyril's Dad, now annoyed. "Look, I've actually been down this road before and if you don't stop them then I'll have to, and it will become a no-win scenario for everyone. The boys won't like what happens, their parents and the school certainly won't like what happens, and I could possibly end up in a spot of bother.

"But rest assured that if I have to take care of the matter myself and do end up in some sort of bother, I'll certainly make sure the papers get hold of it and that the name of your school features prominently. It's pretty despicable, really, picking on a kid like mine, or any kid for that matter. I'm sure the public would agree with me." He paused, then added: "I'll leave it with you, then," and hung up.

The deputy head was annoyed. How dare that man ring up and threaten them like that, she thought. Everyone knew the school was one of the best in town, scholastically and otherwise, and adhered to the strictest Christian principles.

Shaking her head, she decided there must be some mistake. She wouldn't bother the principal with the complaint, or even follow it up herself. It would demean the school to even contemplate that their students would behave in such a manner. She put the matter out of her mind and carried on with her ever-pressing agenda.

So poor old Cyril still kept getting the raw end of the deal on the bus. He was bullied Tuesday morning and Wednesday morning, and it became obvious to his Dad that the school had done nothing about the problem.

Dad decided he needed to be a bit cunning this time. He wanted to be absolutely sure of his facts before taking any action. So he asked his daughter Kylie to get on the bus at the stop before Cyril did. She was to sit right at the back and not let him see her, which was highly unlikely anyway because his eyesight was very poor at the best of times, especially at longer distances. She was to observe everything without doing anything and just make sure the boys were from the school Cyril and old Bert had said they were.

She wasn't actually supposed to get involved at all if the bullying started. But when it did, she just couldn't stop herself. She jumped up and shamed the bullies, giving them a tongue-lashing and warning them to leave Cyril alone. She copped a fair bit of lip and not a few threats back in return, but didn't let that worry her at all.

Cyril was thankful for the distraction and didn't even bother to wonder why his sister had been there. He was just delighted to get off the bus with no more hassles. Kylie stayed on the bus until all the boys got off, then followed them and watched them walk into their school. No mistake there, she thought, it was that snobby Christian school all right, with the well-publicised and oft-quoted motto and principles. Poofters' paradise, the kids at her school had all called it in her day.

She crossed the road to catch another bus in to work. She'd tell Dad tonight. He was off work tomorrow and she wouldn't like to be in those boys' shoes if they bullied Cyril again. Sparks could fly if

Dad got angry. Well, she'd warned them. There'd be no telling what he would do. It might be a pretty fiery Friday morning if he got upset. She almost wished she could be there.

The next day, Cyril's Dad went off in the car early without saying a word, parked in a side street and caught the bus at the stop before Cyril's. As expected, Cyril didn't even notice him sitting right at the back of the bus, cap pulled down low over his forehead and sunglasses on.

Three boys from the Christian school got on noisily at the next stop, joined by several others at the next few stops.

Just when Cyril's Dad was beginning to think his trip had been in vain, it started. "Hey, there's the four-eyed freak again," one of them called out loudly.

They all laughed, then another chipped in: "Yeah, you four-eyed, dopey-looking halfwit." That really started the ball rolling. They strived to outdo each other with insults, as though trying to see who could make the group laugh the most.

Cyril's Dad sat still and quiet, uneasily and reluctantly. Silently, he urged himself to remain cool and try to remember each of the bullies for future identification. His plan was to follow the boys to their school and point them out to their teachers, although it was increasingly hard to sit quiet and do nothing while his son was being subject to such abuse. He was proud of Cyril, though, because he was doing exactly what he had told him to do – looking woodenly ahead and totally ignoring the insults.

Cyril's stop was coming up next, much to his Dad's relief. He'd had real trouble restraining himself while his son had been putting up with all the verbals. It's only words, it's only words, he'd had to keep repeating to himself; ironically, it was the exact same advice he'd given to Cyril.

Cyril rang the bell, stood up and moved eagerly toward the rear exit, keen to get off and away from his tormentors. His father was pleased, too. Cyril had borne up well under the abuse and was finally going to get away from it. But then came the last straw. As Cyril went past, one of the boys ducked out of his seat and gave him a solid push. That didn't really cause too much harm because Cyril managed to grab the pole at the top of the stairs. But he was still off balance when another boy gave him further push, just as the bus was stopping. Cyril lurched awkwardly down the stairwell and only just managed to stop himself slamming heavily into the doors, which had already begun to open.

All the bullies were laughing, loudly, almost maniacally. Still off balance, Cyril suddenly heard an almighty roar and looked up. To his complete and utter surprise, he saw his Dad erupting among the bullies. Bodies seeming to be flying everywhere. Where had Dad come from? Cyril wondered.

Dad was so angry, he'd grabbed the two boys who'd done the pushing by the front of their shirts, one in each hand, and lifted them off their feet and was now shaking them violently. It reminded the bewildered Cyril of the time PD had caught a rat in the park and shook it to break its neck. Dad threw the two boys back into their seats with a solid thump, slapped them both solidly across the face and then turned to the rest. "You horrible, cowardly lot!" he bellowed. "It takes six of you to gang up on a Down Syndrome kid! Well, I'll fix the whole lot of you up and we'll see how you like it!"

He slapped each face solidly in turn with an open palm, then turned back to the first two, still cowering in their seats and shedding frightened tears. "If any of you even think about picking on this kid, or any other kid for that matter, and I hear about it, I'll come back and you'll rue that day for the rest of your life!" He paused for effect, then roared: "Have you got it?"

There was no answer from the by-now completely cowed and weeping brigade of ex-bullies. "Have! You! Got! It!" he roared again. Six frightened heads were nodding rapidly when the driver finally arrived on the scene. Like the rest of the passengers still glued to their seats, he had been shocked motionless at the sudden and furious assault.

"Hey mister," the driver began, "you can't slap kids around like th–." Dad cut him off abruptly: "If you'd been going your job properly, mate, I wouldn't have had to."

He turned back to the boys and pointed his finger at them. "Don't forget! If this ever happens again, you'll rue the living day you see me again!"

Suddenly calm again, he turned and walked slowly down the steps to Cyril, who'd been looking on in utter amazement. He took him by the hand. "Come on, son," he said. "I'll walk you to school."

"Hey! What's your name!" the driver yelled. Neither father nor son took the slightest bit of notice as they walked slowly away. The driver shrugged his shoulders and went back to his seat, wondering what he should do with the bawling kids. Call the cops, perhaps? But that would make him late again, and he didn't really need yet another complaint about that, did he? Somewhat reluctantly, he got on the radio to inform his base of the goings-on.

When Cyril arrived home from school that afternoon, he was not entirely surprised to see a police car parked outside their house. When he entered the kitchen, Dad was sitting at the table talking to two police officers, a man and a woman.

Someone on the bus had recognized Cyril, knew where he lived and informed the police. Dad had already been taken down to the station, charged with six counts of assault, and bailed.

Cyril didn't really know what it all meant but knew it wasn't good as he listened to Dad talking to the police. "What about those brats assaulting my son," Dad was saying. "He could very well have fallen off that bus, you know. I was only defending him."

"That's all very well, Mr McGonagle," said the policewoman. "The principal of the school said if you had only laid a complaint, they would have handled it, and then there would have been no need for you to do what you did."

"I bloody well did," Dad said indignantly. "I laid a complaint to that useless deputy principal, over a week ago now it was. All she could bloody well say was that with their high standards, the students would never do a thing like that. And she obviously did nothing about it at all, because they still kept hassling the boy."

"The principal didn't seem to know anything about that when we spoke to him this morning. In fact, he never mentioned it at all," replied the policewoman.

"Well I definitely rang, a Mrs Boyd, I think she said her name was, and the boy was still harassed every day this week, and put in a potentially dangerous situation today as well. If I'm going to be charged, then I want those boys charged with assault as well.

"You go and ask her if I rang her," he continued irately. "And, oh yeah, tell her that if I go to court, I'll make damn sure the newspapers and media hear about the story as well. That'll look good in the news, won't it? Six pupils from their snobby school ganging up on a kid with Down Syndrome."

"I can understand the frustration you feel, sir," said the policewoman sympathetically. "But we can't really charge those boys with anything. They're under age. You'd have been far better off contacting the school or ringing us."

Dad shook his head wearily. "I say again, I did contact the school and they did absolutely nothing. And as for the police, well, just a few months ago my neighbour got home late one night to find his house had been burgled. He rang your guys and they didn't even bother to turn up till the next day. More urgent cases to attend to, they said. So what chance would I have had to get a result through you?"

"We do have our priorities and staff shortages too, sir," said the policeman rather defensively. "But the fact remains that you did commit an offence, no matter what the provocation, and you have been duly charged."

"That's fine," said Dad. "I'll have my day in court, then. But I'll make damn sure it's well publicised. And you can tell the school that, too."

"Yes sir, we will," said the policewoman, looking sympathetically at Cyril and feeling just a little sorry for his father, who had probably only done what a lot of other fathers would have done in similar circumstances.

"You won't do anything stupid now, will you, like doing a runner, or going after those kids again?" she asked.

"Where the hell would I go," came the snorted reply. "I'll defend the bloody charges and make as much noise as I can while I'm doing it, and you can tell the school that as long as their little angels leave my boy alone, then I'll leave them alone."

Both officers stood up. "Thank you for being so open with us, sir," the man said. " No doubt you will be hearing from us soon."

"Well, I can't say I'm really looking forward to it. But then I suppose you do have your job to do, too," said Dad. Then he surprised Cyril by shaking hands with the officers.

Outside, the policeman turned to his companion and said: "You know, that man's really stuck between a rock and a hard place. The actual assaults were at the minor end of the scale with not much real harm done, and perhaps even a lesson learnt for some. I might have even done the same thing if it had been my kid."

The policewoman just shook her head sadly and said: "I know."

Cyril wasn't bothered at all by the bullies over the following week and he soon began to enjoy his morning bus trips again. One thing about Down kids, they forget things quickly, especially bad things. For the first few days following the incident, he noticed some of the other kids looking at him and talking. Then a few of the girls began to say hullo. Some even knew his name, which was cool.

Usually, most of the other kids didn't really like to be seen talking to him outside of school, especially when their friends were around. He didn't really know why. He knew he was sort of different somehow, but he still liked talking and playing with the other kids.

After a few more days one girl, Ruth, even began to sit and talk to him on the bus, which was really choice. She told him she hadn't liked those boys either, that they were just bullies and she was glad his Dad had done something about it. He only ever saw a couple of those boys again, the rest never reappeared on the bus. The two that did sat as far away from him as possible and wouldn't even look his way.

He saw old Bert sometimes and sat with him if he could. They talked – well, Bert did most of the talking. Actually, it was yelling, really, and he spat a bit as well. Cyril sometimes thought that perhaps he should wear a raincoat when talking to Bert. Bert told him he'd heard what his father had done and that he was a hard man but he'd done the right thing. He said it was his Dad's army service, which he hardly ever spoke about, that made him do what he had to do. But Cyril wondered if his Dad really had done the right thing. Some official mail had arrived from the police and Dad had to go to court next month. He really hoped Dad wasn't going to get into too much trouble.

A week or so later, the local community newspaper ran an article about the incident under the headline UNPROVOKED ATTACK STUNS LOCAL SCHOOL. It said a male passenger had made a seemingly unprovoked attack on several students from the local Christian school on a bus, manhandling and slapping them around.

The students had become very distressed, it went on to say, and several had had to go home. The school was now very concerned about how and why this terrible and most upsetting incident had occurred, and they wanted the book thrown at the offender. The article ended saying that police had charged a man with six counts of assault and a court appearance was due next month.

Jim the publican spotted it and showed it to old Bert. "That's not bloody right," old Bert spluttered in a voice several decibels higher than his normal shout. "What's the number of that paper? I'm going to set them straight."

After several abortive attempts Jim finally got a hold of the right person and handed the phone to Bert, who related his side of the story. By the time he was finished, the phone was thoroughly wet. The reporter pricked up her ears on hearing Bert's side of the story. Good human interest story here, with a Down Syndrome boy. Unfortunately, neither Jim nor old Bert knew Cyril's surname or where he lived. Jim suggested she try the police. The reporter did just that and was lucky enough to be put straight on to the policewoman who was handling the case, the same one who had been round to Cyril's place.

Conveying sympathy for Cyril's Dad, she confirmed that a Down Syndrome boy had been bullied by students from the school mentioned in the paper, and on more than a few occasions. The father claimed he had rung the school and complained but because the bullying hadn't stopped, he had then taken the law into his own hands. No, she couldn't disclose the boy's name or where he lived, but if the reporter contacted the school the boy went to, which she was happy to name, perhaps they might be able to help.

The reporter was now hot on the trail. Her editor agreed there was a good story here. And why hadn't the Christian school mentioned the father's complaint in their first interview? The reporter needed to talk to both the schools concerned and the father of the Down Syndrome boy. With a great deal of enthusiasm, she started making phone calls.

Although worried about the upcoming court case, Cyril's Dad was happy that at least things were back to normal for his son. Cyril was getting to school without being hassled and he now even had friends on the bus.

Dad had cooled off since the incident. He hadn't bothered going to the papers as he had threatened, not even when he saw the article in the local rag. He accepted, somewhat sheepishly, that he had screwed up by going off half-cocked. But he was still going to plead not guilty to the charges. He'd have his day in court and maintain he was only defending his son. He would make sure to point out that his son had no idea how to defend himself and especially against a mob of ignorant, cruel children who should, according to their school anyway, have known better. He hoped the judge wouldn't be too harsh and just fine him.

He knew, though, that the maximum penalty for each of the six charges was a $6000 fine or 18 months' jail. So prison was a real possibility. Dad had heard that the school's lawyer, not uncoincidentally a parent and trustee, was going to push for as heavy a penalty as possible.

The policewoman had told Cyril's Dad he needed a lawyer, and even suggested a woman who had a very good reputation. As far as the officer was concerned, there was no reason to disbelieve him when he said he had made a complaint to the school. She wondered why they hadn't acted on it, and why they hadn't mentioned it. It was something a lawyer could argue to the judge – it showed the defendant had tried to do something about the situation, and if the school had acted on the complaint, the offences may not have occurred.

Cyril's school would not give the reporter his name and address, even when she visited the principal personally. He agreed, reluctantly, to take her business card and pass it on to Cyril's Dad, letting him decide whether to contact her. Cyril's Dad studied the reporter's business card. "What do you reckon, Cyril? Shall we talk to the newspaper?" Cyril shrugged. He didn't take much notice of newspapers. "Oh well, it can't do any more damage and it may help us, I suppose," said Cyril's Dad. He rang the number and left a message for the reporter, who was out of the office.

She got hold of Dad when he awoke the following afternoon, having done a night shift. He confirmed what Bert had said, that three different people had witnessed the bullying on separate occasions and he had rung the school himself the week before the incident and laid a complaint with the deputy principal. He also gave her the name of the person he had spoken to, the date and the approximate time the complaint had been laid.

The reporter hung up the phone. She was about to ring the Christian school for further comment, but then thought better of it. Perhaps a personal visit would be more appropriate – they would be less likely to fob her off. Eagerly, she headed for her car. The man may be guilty of assault, she thought, but the school had certainly been remiss in not acting on the complaint. And it sounded like there had been a fair bit of provocation.

Cyril's Dad was really impressed with the lawyer. The policewoman had been absolutely right. She really knew her stuff. And she wanted to talk to Cyril too, at home, though, with him, his wife or both of them present. He had no problem with that, although he didn't know how much use Cyril would be. He always forgot things very quickly, got flustered easily and if you asked him what he'd done that day, he'd usually have forgotten or have trouble putting it into words. If you asked him what he'd had for lunch, though, he would remember that. But Cyril's Dad was prepared to try anything. He had been dismayed when informed of the penalty he might well have to pay for the assaults, but he was trying not to show this in front of the family. The family might be able to handle a stiff fine, but the possibility of jail really worried him. He hadn't factored that into the equation.

When Cyril went down to the pub with Dad the following Sunday, everyone made a big fuss of him. They bought him Coke and chips and he had half a dozen games of pool, winning the lot. Eventually even he began to suspect that some of his opponents were letting him win, but it was still a lot of fun. Everyone was outraged when they learned that his Dad had been charged and when the two finally left to go home, the place was still buzzing with outrage and conjecture.

The next edition of the community newspaper duly appeared, with a different slant on the assault story. Without naming Cyril or his Dad, it quoted Bert's account of the bullying on the bus, and noted that Cyril's Dad had rung the school with a complaint that had not been acted on.

Of the complaint by Dad, the Christian school was reported as saying there had been "a terrible breakdown of communication, a clerical error, and measures were being put in place to ensure that this could never happen again".

"Notwithstanding that, though," the principal was quoted as saying, "a serious assault on some of our pupils had taken place and the person committing it should still answer to the full weight of the law." Of the bullying allegations, he said: "Of course it is simply appalling to think that any of our children would do such a thing. The allegation will be investigated and I will speak to the whole school about the matter."

Cyril's Dad snorted when he read the principal's comments. "The arrogant beggars," he said. "They didn't believe me in the first place. That's why they did nothing about it."

He was already resigned to the fact that he would more than likely be convicted and hoped for not too heavy a fine, still shuddering to think that he might get even worse. He kept himself busy over the following month, doing extra shifts whenever he could, just in case, as he told everyone, "I get an all-expenses-paid holiday".

He pretended to be upbeat and unconcerned about it all, especially for Cyril's benefit, because he knew stress or trouble upset him and that he could somehow sense when things just weren't quite right. He'd mentioned the spot of bother he was in to one of the more decent supervisors at work, who had said a conviction may well have some bearing on his continued employment, as all staff were required to have a police clearance. The supervisor had suggested they wait and see what happened before they did anything about it. But it was just another source of worry for Cyril's Dad as he waited for his day in court. With all the fuss being raised by the school, he was now beginning to think that he might be quite heavily punished.

In his own mind it was him, on his own, against the school and the full weight of the law, and he didn't think he had much of a chance at all. He didn't even think about all the friends he and Cyril had down at the pub. So he didn't know that Bert, still totally outraged at what had occurred, had come up with an idea. Jim the publican lent brains and organisation, finding out where Cyril lived and making contact with his Mum when the others weren't home. A plot was hatched, with the decision not to tell either of them – especially Cyril, because he had never quite learnt how to keep a secret.

Cyril really liked the lady lawyer. She'd gently asked him a lot of questions at home, most of which only required a yes or no answer. She also let him put any longer answers he'd had to give into his own words, without hurrying him along at all. When she'd asked him if he'd do exactly the same thing in court, in front of the judge to help Dad, he'd said yes. He didn't know what a court or a judge did really, but if it would help Dad, of course he'd do it. He somehow sensed that Dad wasn't feeling quite as confident about the outcome as he made out, and that he was putting on a brave face.

Court day. Cyril's Dad was apprehensive and not really half as confident as he made out in front of the rest of the family at home in the morning. He had a good look around before he left, too, giving PD a good pat. It might be a while before he saw him again.

He approached the courthouse with his head down, hands in pockets, deep in morose thought, not paying too much attention to his surroundings. It was a Friday again, he mused to himself. Everything seemed to happen on bloody Fridays.

There seemed to be quite a crowd milling around outside the courthouse as he gathered himself and prepared to enter. Suddenly, a group of people right outside the main doors began chanting loudly. He looked up and immediately recognized the six boys from the bus, spotless in their school uniforms and looking absolutely angelic, as if butter wouldn't melt in their mouths. They were being anxiously ushered inside by parents or school officials and were obviously there to give evidence against him.

But the crowd lined up at the door were chanting something, it sounded like "Bullies, bullies, shame, shame". There it was again: "Bullies, bullies, shame, shame."

Cyril's Dad blinked and stared at the chanting crowd in utter surprise. There wasn't a face among them that he didn't know. There was old Bert, the last of the summer wine, along with Pete, Jim, Ann, Kim, Jerry, Dennis and at least half a dozen or so others from the pub whose names he didn't know. They were fair giving those school kids a real mouthful.

A sudden flash of light startled him and he noticed the local rag's reporter there as well, along with a photographer. And not only that, but a TV crew as well.

"What the heck's going on here?" he said somewhat bewilderedly, directing the question at his crowd of friends. Old Bert emerged and strode up to him, clapping him on the arm. "Ya didn't think we were going to leave ya ta face it on ya own, did ya?" he yelled, spitting right in Dad's ear. "It's not right, ya know, I'm gonna give evidence for ya and there's a special witness here for ya too. Come on, let's go in."

The two entered the courthouse amid clapping and cheering from the assembled group of friends from the pub. They all sat down in the foyer to wait for the case to be called, talking loudly among themselves and earning rebukes from the harassed and busy court staff. There was no sign of the students. They'd obviously been taken elsewhere out of sight to wait, which was probably just as well.

Cyril's Dad was puzzled. What were all his mates from the pub doing here? It was good of them to come and lend support and he could probably use Bert's evidence of prior bullying to his advantage. But he wasn't really that sure if it would do any good at all.

All the same, he didn't feel quite so apprehensive or alone now. He had friends supporting him, and that was a good feeling. He wondered who the surprise witness was. Oh well, we'll find out soon enough I suppose, he thought, then looked up. All the people from the pub gave him the thumbs up with big encouraging smiles. He managed a smile in return. At least they're confident, he thought. But he certainly wasn't.

Nearly another hour of sitting nervously in the foyer passed before the case was finally called. Dad entered the courtroom and was immediately surprised to see his wife and Cyril sitting right up the front, close to his lawyer. How had they got in without him seeing? He'd told them they might as well stay at home. If he was going to be found guilty, he would have preferred that they didn't see it. What were they doing here?

All the pub people then filed in and old Bert came right on up the aisle and whispered something to Dad's lawyer. Well, it wasn't really a whisper, that was just about impossible for Bert. It was more of a rumble and despite the pickle he was in, Cyril's Dad had to have a bit of a giggle when he noticed the lawyer wiping the side of her face afterwards.

Soon the clerk of the court told them all to stand while the judge came in, then when they were eventually allowed to sit Dad's name was called and he stood while the charges were read out. His lawyer immediately entered a not guilty plea.

The prosecution lawyer opened. He looked gravely around the courtroom and then began: "Your Honour, the prosecution will prove undeniably that these most disturbing assaults by Mr McGonagle did indeed take place on the six school children. As well as the evidence of the six victims, there are various other witnesses statements, all the people present on the bus, for instance, so I would like it duly noted that the defendant's plea of not guilty is a waste of the court's valuable time. Which fact should, Your Honour, be remembered when passing sentence.

"These charges are serious ones and should be severely punished to send out a strong message to the public that this sort of behaviour will not be tolerated."

He paused for a breath, looked dramatically around the courtroom over the top of his glasses, then continued: "Children should be able to travel to school unmolested and in complete safety. Any talk of provocation does not detract from the seriousness of these assaults, and indeed the fact that the defendant actually travelled on the bus at all demonstrates a certain amount of premeditation, which in my mind makes the offences even worse.

"Your Honour, once we have demonstrated unequivocally that these offences did indeed occur we would ask that the strongest message possible be sent to the public that this sort of behaviour will simply not be tolerated in our society."

Pointing to Cyril's Dad, he continued: "The defendant, this, this child basher, should be punished as severely as the law will allow."

There was a general stir in the court as the lawyer finished his opening speech, stared dramatically and sternly at Cyril's Dad, then sat down. The judge rapped his gavel twice. "Order, order," he called and looked at the defence lawyer.

She slowly rose, composed herself and began to address the judge and the courtroom.

"Your Honour," she said, "I would like to emphasise and endorse something my learned colleague has just said." She paused theatrically for a few seconds, then continued: "That children should be able to travel to school unmolested and in complete safety." She paused again, then repeated: "Children should be able to travel to school unmolested, and in complete safety."

The court was quiet as everyone took in these words. Then she repeated them a third time: "Children should be able to travel to school unmolested and in complete safety."

After another long pause, she began again: "Your Honour, my client does not deny the fact that he," a pregnant pause, "did manhandle the complainants." There was another murmur in the court and the judge called for silence. "In fact, Your Honour," she continued, "he freely admits it."

There was another stir, which the judge ignored this time. "In defence, Your Honour," yet another pause, "in defence of his son's right to get to school unmolested and in complete safety, as so correctly stated by my colleague."

Some of the pub people let out a huge cheer and were immediately reprimanded by the judge, who said he'd have them removed if they interrupted again.

"All I ask, Your Honour, is that you listen to my client's story and ask yourself," with a gesture to the courtroom, "everyone here should ask themselves, what would you have done if this was your son?

"Had the complaint laid by the defendant with the school some seven days before the event took place been acted upon, it would surely never have come to this. We also contend that the charges of assault are far too serious for the actual events that took place."

The courtroom went quiet as everyone digested what she had just said and the lawyer sat down pleased with the way her opening address had gone.

The prosecution lawyer frowned. She'd taken points off him there, he thought, but still, the defendant had admitted the charges so it should be an easy victory now.

He stood and addressed the court. "Your Honour, as the defendant has admitted committing the offences and I have no wish to put the victims through the anguish of recounting the assaults, I rest my case."

The judge acknowledged this statement and asked the defence lawyer to continue.

Bert was quickly called, sworn in and asked for his evidence, which he gave in his normal loud voice, asking for several of the questions to be repeated and making the audience smile. He was very particular in his claim that he had seen Cyril actually assaulted and put in a potentially very dangerous situation.

He also confirmed that the boys in court were the same ones who had assaulted Cyril, and he recognised them from waiting at the bus stop and observing their generally bad behaviour then and on previous journeys.

This didn't go down too well with the prosecution, whose lawyer immediately rose. "Objection, Your Honour," he called. "The complainants aren't the ones up on charge. This evidence has nothing to do with the case." The judge agreed, but everyone else smiled. Old Bert had certainly got his point across anyway. And the prosecution lawyer didn't cross-examine him.

At that stage, Cyril's Dad was expecting to be called next, but was completely dumbfounded when Cyril was called instead. He had thought that if necessary, they might have just used a statement from him and not put him in the box. So this came as a complete surprise.

The lawyer escorted Cyril to the witness box herself talking quietly and encouragingly to him all the way. He was sworn in, although his Dad was pretty sure he wouldn't have known what it was all about anyway.

The lady lawyer took him slowly through his evidence as she had done at home, mostly yes or no questions, leading him to a certain extent, although the opposition raised no objection. The prosecution lawyer was well aware of the sympathy that the Down Syndrome boy could evoke and did not want to look to be unfeeling by jumping down his throat. Anyway, he thought, a conviction is a certainty, so he let it go.

Cyril was doing really well. He was a bit shaky and nervous at the start, with everyone looking at him. But the lawyer soon got him settled down. The questions were all easy, and he'd answered them all before anyway.

It was all going exceptionally well until they got to the bit where the first boy had pushed him. Suddenly she threw him to the wolves by asking him to describe in his own words what had happened. Cyril was totally puzzled at this. It hadn't been like this at home. The nice lady had asked the questions and he'd just mostly had to say yes or no.

He looked at Mum, then over at Dad, who nodded and gave him an encouraging smile. That's right, he had to help Dad. So slowly and hesitantly, he began: "I – I was getting off the bus . . . one boy push me . . . I hold the rail," he said.

The lawyer nodded. "What happened then?" she asked gently.

"Other boy push me . . . I fall down stairs." Cyril hesitated for a few more seconds, obviously trying to remember, then burst out indignantly: "I nearly fall out of bus!"

The lawyer nodded encouragingly again. This was all good stuff. "After you nearly fell out of the bus, what happened then?"

Cyril hesitated for at least 10 more seconds and she thought he hadn't understood the question. She was just going to repeat it again, when he said quietly: "My Dad save me again."

The lawyer stopped, motionless, sensing that somehow something important had just been offered. "Can you say that again please, Cyril?" she asked. "Only louder this time."

"My Dad save me again," he repeated in a loud voice.

She hesitated, then turned to the judge and said: "His Dad saved him again, Your Honour. This boy believes his Dad's action saved him."

There was a long pause before she continued: "Your Honour, is it not the right of every child to be defended by their parents?" Another pause. "Conversely, is it not the duty of every parent to defend their children? I strongly suggest that the only crime my client is guilty of is defending his child, and what true parent would not want to do that?"

The question, asked with a raised voice hung in the air for a few seconds, then spontaneously cheering and clapping broke out in the court with cries of "hear, hear," mostly from the pub people. The judge ordered everyone to be quiet then asked the defence lawyer: "Have you finished with this witness?"

She nodded and turned to the prosecution lawyer who, seeing he was going to gain nothing in talking to the boy, flagged the opportunity away.

The judge then surprised everyone by directing a question to Cyril himself: "Cyril, why did you say your father saved you again?"

There was a long silence before Cyril started: "Before...before...some boys hit me when I coming home from school and my Dad...hit them back and make them stop."

Oh no, the lawyer thought. That's torn it. We didn't really need that to come out.

"Did that stop them, Cyril?" the judge asked. "They never hit me again," replied Cyril.

"Does your father always look after you?" the judge then asked. "My Dad always looking after me," came the reply, Cyril looking intently at his father with a big smile.

"Thank you, Cyril," said the judge. "You have done really well and given me much to think about."

At that stage his Dad was finally expecting to be called. But his lawyer decided not to. She had sensed something in what Cyril had said and also in the judge's input, and thought it would be a good time to rest her case.

Each lawyer was then asked to make a closing address.

The prosecution lawyer reasoned to himself that while he had lost a bit of ground to his opposite, a conviction was still a certainty. He adopted an almost conciliatory tone.

"Bullying (not assaulting) any child, let alone a handicapped one, by others who should have known better is indeed a despicable act," he said with a stern look at the complainants, several of whom squirmed visibly.

"But," he continued, "we should not lose sight of the fact that a serious crime has been committed here and if the defendant, who has seemingly committed a similar assault previously, is let off lightly, it will send a message to the public in general that such assaults will be tolerated, Your Honour, I would humbly suggest that in this violent era we live in, that is entirely the wrong message to be sending." He nodded to the judge and sat down.

Dad's lawyer kept it light and quick also, perceiving that she'd already had her definitive moment with Cyril, and not wanting to lose any of the impact of that.

"Your Honour," she said," I would just like to reiterate my colleague's own words, it is indeed the right of every child to get to school unmolested and in complete safety. I also believe it is every parent's duty to defend their children to the best of their ability.

"My client is only guilty of doing what should come naturally to every parent, and if for a few seconds he lost his cool under extreme provocation, can anyone blame him?" she asked. Gesturing to the complainants, she added: "There doesn't seem to be any lasting damage done."

She paused for 10 long seconds then pointed dramatically to Cyril. "Your Honour," she said. "The last thing this child needs in his life is a father who will not defend and protect him, or indeed," with another pause, "a father who is not around ready to defend or protect him. I humbly ask you to take this into account when considering your verdict and sentence."

She sat down to another outbreak of clapping and cheering which the judge eventually managed to silence. "I will retire to my chambers to consider my decision," he said. "While the actual commission of the crime is evident, some compelling points have been raised for consideration." The court rose while the judge retired.

Outside, everyone was talking 90 to the dozen, nervous cigarettes were lit and people walked up and down, too tension-filled to be still. The judge seemed to be taking forever but everyone reckoned that this was a good sign for the defendant. The longer the better. The reporter and photographer were still there, as was the TV crew. Passers-by were stopping in, attracted by the crowd. It seemed there was a lot of public interest in the case.

Elsewhere in the court building, the prosecution lawyer was feeling his first misgivings. What had seemed like a cut-and-dried case, with a sure conviction, suddenly didn't seem to be so anymore. Had he taken too much for granted? Maybe. Well, it was too late now, that was for sure.

For his part, Cyril's Dad, was very nervous and had an exceedingly dry mouth. But he was resigned to whatever the outcome. That lawyer had done a bloody good job, he thought, and he was proud of Cyril. Whatever happened, he must tell him that.

The time dragged on and it was more than two long hours before they were finally called back in. Cyril's Dad stood, heart in his mouth, awaiting his fate as the judge began delivering his verdict.

"I have found this case particularly difficult," he said. "Not in determining the guilt or innocence of the defendant, but in how much the special circumstances surrounding them actually led to the offences being committed.

"It is perhaps a pity," he said, with an admonishing look at the school party, "that the initial complaint wasn't investigated when it was received, instead of being, as I understand it, so totally disbelieved. If it had been investigated and acted on, there is no doubt in my mind that we wouldn't have found ourselves in this courtroom today.

"Nevertheless," and he turned to Cyril's Dad, "it is by your own admission that you committed the assaults, and I find you guilty on all charges."

Cyril's Dad swallowed nervously. Well, he'd expected that.

The judge looked sternly at him before continuing: "You are sentenced to one month's jail, on each of the charges." Cyril's Dad's heart missed a beat and his supporters were all quiet, stunned. Six months in jail. Hell.

But the judged continued: "The sentences to be served concurrently." Only one month in jail. Well, that wasn't quite as bad, Cyril's Dad thought.

"However," continued the judge, still looking directly at Dad, "I suspend the sentence on a 12-month bond of good behaviour, because the law, the law, should not deprive this boy of his father."

There was a short, stunned silence, then the whole courtroom erupted into cheering. This time the judge did have some difficulty in getting control back.

When he did finally manage to silence everyone, he looked at Cyril's Dad with a stern unblinking gaze: "Mr McGonagle, you are to be commended for your efforts in protecting your son. You have obviously done a similar act previously and got away with it, but this time you have found yourself up on charges.

"I would like to make it perfectly clear that if I ever find you up in front of me again on similar charges, you can expect no mercy. If in the future incidents like this do re-occur, I urge you, go to the schools, go to the parents, go to the papers, go to the police if need be, but, do not, do not, take the law into your own hands. Do I make myself perfectly clear?"

"Yes, Your Honour," came the very sheepish reply.

Suddenly it was all over. The tension was gone and the court rose while the judge retired, then immediately broke into an excited happy chatter, while the anxious courtroom ushers tried to hustle everybody out. They were already far behind time. This case had taken far longer than expected.

Outside, Cyril made a dash to his father, followed by his Mum. He didn't really understand what had occurred, but with all the cheering coming from their friends he suspected it must be good. And it was.

His Dad was shaking hands with the lawyer. "You did a bloody good job," he said. "It wasn't me," she said, indicating Cyril. "It was Cyril who made the difference."

Dad was rubbing his hand in Cyril's hair when old Bert and the rest of their friends arrived, swarming all over them, shaking hands and slapping backs. Cyril thought it was all so exciting.

The group edged their way slowly downstairs, where the reporter and TV crew awaited them. When asked for her comment on the verdict, their lawyer said: "This is an example of justice at its best, tempered with mercy and common sense, and it makes one proud to be a part of it."

The prosecution lawyer was not quite so happy, however. "We are upset at the light sentence and the fact that despite the guilty verdict, costs were not awarded. We will definitely be considering an appeal."

The reporter chased down the principal of the Christian school and asked: "Would you have wanted an obviously special boy to be without his father?" The principal spat the dummy at that, refusing to comment and charging after his students, who were being hastily led away from the noisy throng by their anxious minders.

The reporter for the local rag was invited back to the pub with the rest of them where she could ask all the questions she wanted to. The lawyer was also invited. She'd love to, she said, but simply had too much work to do. The policeman and policewoman passed by. They didn't say anything but they smiled at Dad and Cyril.

And Cyril? He was happy because his Mum and Dad were happy. He also knew his Dad would always stick up for him no matter what. And that was exactly what the judge hadn't wanted to take away from him.

Yep, it looked like Fridays were going to be good days again.

MORE BMS BOOKS

Enjoyed this book? The following list of books is available from BMS Books.

A Soldier's Life by Lou Geraets

My Life…the Meanderings of Pop Knill by Lou Geraets

The Forgotten by Sarah Groot

Forestry, People and Places – Selected Writings from Five Decades by Dennis Richardson

Demons Inside My Mind – Life with Anorexia – Jenna Oldham

For more information, contact:
BMS Books
5 High Street, Glenholme
Rotorua 3010
New Zealand
Email: ms@bms.co.nz
URL: www.bms.co.nz
Tel: 64-7-349 4107